COLORADO RENEGADE

Colorado Territory Series Book III

JOHN LEGG

WOLFPACK
PUBLISHING
— EST 2013 —

WOLFPACK
PUBLISHING
— EST 2013 —

Colorado Renegade

Paperback Edition
Copyright © 2021 John Legg

Wolfpack Publishing
5130 S. Fort Apache Road, 215-380
Las Vegas, NV 89148

wolfpackpublishing.com

Paperback ISBN: 978-1-64734-750-5
eBook ISBN: 978-1-64734-748-2

COLORADO RENEGADE

PROLOGUE

The old man stopped his horse in front of the adobe house. The place was old, even older than the man, but it was in good condition, as was he. The main part of the house was a little smaller than he remembered, but it had been added to at least twice. The horse corral was still there off to the left against the adobe wall of the compound, and a wood barn, spilling out hay, was behind it, stretching almost to the back wall. A chicken coop near the rear of the house was dangerously close to falling. Several open-faced stalls where blacksmithing, carpentry, and other trades were plied, all seemingly unused now, stood on the right along the east wall. A truck garden took up part of the yard along the left side of the house, and the covered ramada had been incorporated into an addition to the house. Cattle still roamed the fields outside the walls, but the farm fields had been moved over to the land outside the right wall. Several houses remained outside, woodsmoke curling up from them. It all looked pretty much the same as it had forty years ago or so when he was last here except for the Model T parked in front of the garage.

A woman in her mid-forties opened the door and stepped out. She was dark-skinned, with high cheekbones and long, silky black hair streaked with white. She was on the chubby side but still attractive.

"Can I help you, Mister?" she asked, voice pleasant with an unidentifiable accent.

"Hope so, ma'am. I'm looking for John and Matilda."

"John's long passed on."

"Matilda still on this side of the grass?"

"She certainly is. Feisty old woman, that Matilda.

"She around?"

"She went into town with my mother and my daughter. They should be back soon."

"Town?"

"New town sprung up a few miles southwest of here a long time ago. Small place, but it has things we used to have to go to Pueblo for. And it took over much of what we did here with the various trades and such." She paused a moment. "Did you know my grandparents, John and Matilda?" She smiled. "We ain't related, really. I always called them Gramps and Gram anyway."

"I did know 'em, yup. Many years ago. Well, I best be on my way then."

"Wait, Mister...?"

"Elias Prosper."

"I'm Alma Verdugo. You look tired, and the day's getting near to ending. Why don't you put up your horse in the barn and sup with us? Spend the night here, too. There's plenty of room."

"You certain?"

"I am."

"You're not alone, are you? I'd feel rather uncomfortable being in the house alone with you." He grinned. "Even at my age, I still have an eye for a beautiful woman."

She grinned too, both in delight and embarrassment at the compliment. "I'm not alone, considerin' there's a couple of young'uns in the house. The men'll be back before long. You'll be safe from me," she added with a laugh.

Prosper chuckled. "Sounds mighty disappointin', Alma. But I reckon I'll be happy to accept your invitation." He pulled his horse to the side and rode slowly toward the barn. He unsaddled and tended the animal, then ambled to the house, where he rapped on the door.

"Come on in, Elias," Alma hollered.

He did so and took a seat. A boy and a girl, maybe four or five, stared at him. "I ain't about to bite, ya know," he said. "'Course, if you was to come over here, I might scare the bejeebers out of ya." He grinned.

There were a few moments of silence before the girl giggled. The boy stayed silent.

"Well, go on and say hello to Mr. Prosper."

The two children edged up to Prosper, who suddenly reached out and grabbed the boy and swung him into the air. The boy's eyes widened a little in fear, then he howled in delight.

"Me next! Me next!" the girl shouted.

Prosper gave her a ride too, then gave them both

a good tickle, eliciting loud cries of joy.

Finally, Alma said, "That's enough, you two. Go on back to your play and leave Mr. Prosper be."

With grumbles, the two did so.

"Sorry, Mr. Prosper."

"No call to apologize, Alma. I got as much joy out of that few minutes as they did."

Alma smiled and placed a cup of coffee in front of him on the table. He nodded his thanks and drank slowly, watching her as she worked at the stove.

Before long, the sound of a wagon came through to them. "That'll be the menfolk," Alma said.

"Not Matilda and the others?"

"Oh, my, no," Alma responded with a smile. "Matilda and the others are in a small wagon. This one's the men; you can hear it's heavier. Besides, there's some gabbing going on."

A flash of embarrassment crossed Prosper's face. "Sorry, ma'am. My hearing's not quite as good as it was when I was your age."

"I'm sorry, Mr. Prosper," she said with an apologetic smile. "I didn't know."

"You couldn't have known."

"Well, Matilda's about your age, and she's a bit hard of hearing." She laughed a little. "Though I sometimes think she's faking it just to get us shouting."

"That's something Matilda would do, yup. How do you feed 'em all in here? I reckon there's a passel of 'em."

"That's the truth. Some of 'em live outside, thank goodness. I don't know where we'd put 'em all for supper."

"Don't they use that motorized contraption?"

"Some of the men at times. But they can't all fit in it, so they use the wagon to head to work. And Matilda wants nothing to do with it." She grinned.

"Neither do I. My son's got one of 'em." He smiled back. "Do all the men work in the fields? That where they're coming from?"

"No. Some do. Others ply their trades in the town instead of here these days."

A man of about fifty entered the room, asking, "Whose horse is that in the barn, Alma?" He sounded irritated.

Five other men hurried into the room behind him.

"Belongs to Mr. Prosper there," she said, pointing at the visitor.

"Who the hell are you?" the man demanded.

Prosper's hackles rose. "And who the hell are you, sonny?" He stood, hand near the butt of his Starr revolver.

"Oh, shush, Ramon," Alma said. "He's a friend of Matilda's."

"That what he told you?"

"Sí."

"And you believed him?"

"Sí."

"You damn fool."

"That's enough, sonny." Prosper snapped, voice and eyes hard. "That ain't no way to speak to a woman, especially if she's your wife, as I assume she is. Unless you're just an ass who talks to all women that way."

"Why, you..."

"Ramon!" Alma shouted.

"Shut up, woman!" He was about to say more until the click of a Starr revolver's hammer being cocked stopped everyone in the room.

"I've known John and Matilda since long before you were born. And I don't take kindly to men talkin' to a woman in such a way as you've done here. Now, I don't give a hoot what you think of me, but I won't sit here and let you abuse this woman."

"You won't shoot me," Verdugo said with a sneer.

"You willing to risk it? Willing to risk leaving a widow and a couple of orphaned grandchildren?"

With the arguing and the crying of the two little children, who Alma had knelt and held one in each arm, they did not hear the small wagon. Suddenly the door opened—not very far, considering that several men were standing in the way.

"Get out of the doorway, dang it," a woman snapped.

The men moved out of the way, and three women came in, the oldest one growling, "What in heck're you men doin' standin' here in front of the door?" She glared from one to the other until she spotted Prosper. "Well, lookee who's come back after a lifetime away." A great smile lighted up her dark, seamed face. "Put that gun away, Elias."

"You know this man, Matilda?" Ramon asked.

"Of course I do, you durn fool."

As Prosper slid his six-gun back into the holster, two other women pushed their way inside. "What's all the commotion?" the older of the two asked. Then she spotted Prosper.

"Elias?" she whispered. Tears started to flow slowly down her dark cheeks from coal-black eyes.

"This man scaring you?" one of the men asked. He looked ready to have a go at Prosper even though he was unarmed.

Ignoring him, the woman rushed to Prosper, who wrapped his long arms around her and began to stroke her long, now-mostly-gray hair as she held him tight.

"You all right, Smoke?"

She nodded into his chest. "Missed you." She sniffled.

"I missed you, too."

The others stood around, showing various degrees of incredulity. Matilda grinned and pointed at one of the men. "You won't recognize him, but that there fellow is Juan. 'Lives Again' as you were so fond of callin' him."

It was Prosper's turn to be surprised.

"Do I know this man?" Juan said, confused.

Then Alma said, "This is mighty strange. I thought you were here to visit Matilda. And you called Laura Smoke?"

Prosper nodded over Smoke's head.

"But..."

"Oh, quiet, child," Matilda said.

"What the hell is going on here?" one of the other men asked.

"Hush," Matilda said. "Food should be ready. Let's sit to supper, and all will be explained." The youngest of the women hurried to the young children, kissed them on the head, dried their tears, and sent them off to the other side of the room to play while she went to help serve food to the crowd.

The meal was a strained affair, with everyone but Matilda and Smoke Rising anxious to find out what was going on. When the meal finally was over, the dishes cleared, the coffee served, Matilda said, "A long, long time ago, there was a man named Elias Prosper who was travelin' through Colorado when it was still a territory..."

CHAPTER 1

Elias Prosper brought his horse to a stop and listened, unsure what he had heard if anything. Then the sound came again, and he relaxed. It was just a baby gurgling. He started forward, moving slowly, but after a few feet, he stopped once more. If there was a baby ahead, there should be a mother, and therefore, others—likely some warriors, considering where he was. But there was no indication that others were around.

He proceeded cautiously, eyes and ears alert, until he was on the edge of the small lake. He saw no one. Then the baby cooed again. Prosper dismounted and walked toward the sound. He found the child—no more than a few months old, he figured—in a woven basket caught up in some reeds. "Kind of lonely out here like this, ain't it, little one?" he said as he knelt and touched the infant on the cheek with a grubby finger.

Prosper could only wonder what had happened to the child's mother. He sighed. "What'm I gonna do with you, little one?" he asked quietly. He faced a quandary. He could not, of course, leave the infant here to die, but he had no idea where its people were. Realizing he could not keep thinking of the child as "it," he pulled open the cloth swaddling the baby. It was a boy, he found. "Well, young fella," he said as he took the basket in hand and rose, "we'll figure something out."

He hung the basket from his saddle horn and mounted the gelding, then paused for a few moments, trying to decide which way to go. He shrugged and turned north to go around the lake as he'd originally planned. He figured it was most likely he would find some Utes that way, hopefully ones who would know who and where the parents were. He also hoped they would be friendly.

Before long, the baby started fussing. It wasn't too bad at first, but as the noise increased, it began to unnerve Prosper. Mainly he was bothered because he didn't know what to do. He finally stopped and got the small pouch of sugar from his saddlebags. As he rode on, he wet his pinkie, dipped it in the sugar, and let the baby suck on it. That quieted him down.

A few miles up the lake, he came to what had been an Indian camp or maybe a small village. Vultures picked at the remnants of old meat, buckskin, and what seemed to be blood lying around. It appeared to Prosper that they had left quickly. The birds flew off in an explosion of feathers and squawking as he approached. He figured the people had gone off within the past day or maybe two. He thought the baby's parents would be among the Utes who had been here, but why would they leave their infant? Maybe they thought the child had drowned. He hoped the people, including the parents, were within a couple of days' ride. The boy's parents would be overjoyed to have their infant back, he knew.

As he made his small camp that night, Prosper realized he could not keep feeding the child nothing but sugar, though he had no idea what to feed him. There was not a cow, a goat, or even a sheep within hundreds of miles, at least not domesticated. He was not about to try to milk a buffalo or a Rocky Mountain sheep, he thought with a smile. That would be something, trying to hold a fifteen-hundred-pound buffalo cow still while he milked it. He contemplated the situation as he went about his tasks.

By the time he had put on some bacon and coffee, he still hadn't decided, but he did realize as he waited for his dinner that there was a rather strong odor coming from the bundle of boy. "Damn fool," he muttered. He unwrapped the child and placed the naked boy on an extra shirt he carried with him. He took the basket and dumped out the foul grass and moss that had served as an absorbent, put in fresh grass, and wrapped the baby up again.

He sat and tickled the boy's stomach with a finger. "You look a heap more comfortable now, boy," Prosper said. He piled some bacon on a tin plate, and as he began to eat, he noticed the child looking at him. "You can't eat this, boy," he chided gently. Then he looked at the pan, back at the boy, then the pan again. He nodded. It should work, he decided.

When he finished his meal, Prosper got a spoon and scooped up some of the hardened bacon grease. He gently pushed a tiny bit into the baby's mouth from the spoon with his finger. The infant gurgled and smiled, gumming the fat-rich substance. "Like that, do you, boy?" Prosper asked with a grin. The child swallowed several spoonsful before letting out an explosive burp, a giggle, and a fart. Then he fell asleep.

Prosper shook his head in amazement, finished his coffee, and then slept himself.

Breakfast was a repeat of supper for both of them. As he fed the boy, Prosper said, "You need a name, young fellow. How about Solo? Yup, I think that'll do." Prosper refreshed the grass that served as a diaper, packed up his little camp, and moved out.

The day was more of the same: sugar for Solo, jerky for Prosper, water from a canteen for both, more bacon and coffee for Prosper that night, and grease for Solo. And again in the morning.

As he moved north away from the lake, Prosper wondered whether he was ever going to find Solo's people. He could not continue to care for the baby as he had been. For one thing, he was running out of bacon. For another, he wasn't at all sure such a diet was proper for the infant. He figured the boy needed milk, preferably from a woman, not a cow. But there was little to do but press on.

Just before midday, though, he saw signs of an Indian village ahead—thin plumes of smoke from cookfires, and vultures circling on the lookout for scraps of carrion left over from fresh kills or old meals. "Well, young Master Solo, maybe we've found some of your relatives."

A little more than half an hour later, two warriors appeared and stopped, waiting for Prosper. When he was ten feet or so away, he too halted.

"What you want here?" one of the warriors asked in heavily accented English.

"Found this little boy all alone down by that small lake a couple days' ride southwest. Figured he was one of you, and his folks will want him back, thinking he was lost."

The two warriors looked horrified. One spun his horse and galloped off. The other kept a wary eye on Prosper, who was bewildered. Before long, the other warrior came riding back, stopping next to his companion. "You go," he ordered.

Anger flared in Prosper. "I ain't going anywhere 'til I go into that village and find this boy's parents, or else some relatives to care for him if they ain't around."

"No. You go!" the warrior insisted.

"Afraid not, boys." He pulled out a pistol and waved it in the direction of the two Utes. "Lead on." When his blockers made no move to turn around, Prosper thumbed back the hammer. "It'd sure be a poor thing for one of you to die for the sake of this child." There was still hesitation on the part of the warriors, and Prosper was puzzled. It was odd to him that these two would be willing to be shot or killed to prevent him from going into the village. It made no sense. He sighed and uncocked the pistol, though he did not holster it. "All right, then, if you won't take me to the village, one of you go and bring your chief here."

The warriors argued, then the one who had stayed behind the last time raced off.

It was an uncomfortable wait and long, or so it seemed. But finally the chief, escorted by the warrior who had fetched him and two others, along with two older women, arrived.

"Speak," the chief said without preliminary.

"I'm Elias Prosper. Who're you?"

"Iron Sky. Speak."

"You know why I'm here," Prosper said, a little annoyed. "I want to know why you won't take this child off my hands. Even if his folks ain't around, he's still one of yours."

"Bad medicine. You keep. You go."

"Now, just wait a minute there, Chief. Are you saying this child's bad luck?"

"Yes."

"Why? He can't have done anything. Hell, he ain't but a few months is all, best I can tell."

"He is, how white-eyes say, cursed."

"Cursed? What the hell's that mean?"

"He bad medicine," Iron Sky repeated, voice not easing any.

"You said that. What'd this poor little fella do to make him bad medicine?"

Iron Sky hesitated, but one of the women spoke up in halting, barely understandable English. "He woke evil spirits in lake. Arapaho attack us, kill some. Others flee in lake. Die there. We see. He live. We drive enemy away. He float away on own. Anger lake spirit. Make mother, father die in lake. We leave quick before spirit kill more of us."

"You can't believe that hogwash, can you? Any of you?" But their looks told him they could and did. He sat there for a moment, thinking. Solo began to fuss, and without thinking, he wet a finger, dipped it in the pouch of sugar he kept with him all the time now, and held it out to the baby.

The Utes were startled, he noticed, but he wasn't sure it was because they were surprised that a white man—or any man—would do such a thing or if they were horrified that he was caring for the baby they considered cursed. "Well," he finally said, "we got us a dilemma here. This child is one of your people, but you don't want him. He ain't one of my people, and I can't really care for him. Seems to be not much in the way of options."

"Take him," Iron Sky said. "Leave boy in meadow, two miles." He pointed. "Then go."

It took a few moments for the intention to sink into Prosper's brain, and he was incensed. "You mean for me to leave this baby out there in the open for the wolves and coyotes to come and eat him? God-da-yam, that's the most awfullest thing I ever heard. You people're worse than a tribe of devils!" Prosper fought to keep his anger bottled up.

When he finally managed to do so, he said tightly, "This here's what's gonna happen, folks. I'll take this boy with me." He sneered at their looks of relief. "But what you're gonna do is send a woman along with me." His sneer turned to a nasty grin when their faces went from relief to shock. "Don't matter to me if she's young or old, as long as she has milk in her breasts. If she's got her own child, she can bring it, too. She'll have her own horse, and you'll give us enough food and such to last a couple weeks. By then, we should be someplace I can hand the infant to someone who'll care for it proper."

"No, not give woman," the chief said.

"Yup, you will. And when I find a safe place for the boy, I'll send her back to you."

"You keep, I think."

"Nope. Don't want her. Just want a woman along to feed the young'un."

The Utes talked it over in their own language, growing angrier by the moment. Finally Iron Sky looked at Prosper and shook his head. "You go now. We not help. You not make us." He and his people started to turn back toward their village.

Shaking his head in annoyance, he pulled his Starr and shot Iron Sky's horse. The old chief proved more nimble than Prosper would have thought and managed to dismount safely before the horse hit the ground. "Next one's for you, Chief."

The other warriors looked ready to charge, but they were armed only with knives and tomahawks.

"Come on ahead, boys." None of them moved, so Prosper continued, "Now do what I said, Chief. Send one of the women and two of the warriors back to the village and come back with what I asked for. You and the others will stay here with me 'til I get what I want." His voice was hard, unforgiving.

"You'll kill us," Iron Sky said.

"Hell, Chief, if I wanted to kill you, you'd all be

dead now. You send me out a woman heavy with milk, her own horse, and some supplies, and we'll be on our way. Like I said, soon's I find the boy a home, I'll let the woman go."

There was more arguing, then the three designated Utes left. As they did, Prosper warned, "And don't come back with more warriors. Just one of you and that old squaw there bring back the woman and her horse."

Prosper herded the others into a cluster of boulders, where he was safe from attack. He had the warriors dismount and drop their weapons in a pile against one of the rocks. He moved between it and the warriors, and they waited, sweating. The Utes started at Prosper in anger and fear. He stared back in anger and bewilderment at their superstitions. It was a far longer and tenser wait this time, and it gave him time to think. He wondered at the madness of all this. While he did not know but a few Indians, he had heard about their "medicine" but had put it down to superstition. Whites had their superstitions too, but this situation went well beyond that, he thought.

Finally, he heard riders approaching, and he tensed. The old woman led the way into the small clearing circled by the boulders, followed by a young, attractive, slim woman with an empty cradleboard on her back, riding a sad-looking excuse for a pinto, and then the warrior. The young woman looked as if she were riding to her funeral, and Prosper figured she felt exactly that way. The warrior tossed two buckskin sacks on the ground.

"You go now," Iron Sky said, heading for the extra

horse the old woman had brought.

"Whoa, there, pal." Everyone looked at him. Prosper pointed at the young woman who had just ridden in. "Chief, you're gonna ride that fleabag the woman's on and come with me. The young woman'll be ridin' that warrior's horse." He pointed again.

There was more arguing among the Utes, and Iron Horse went to get on the horse he'd intended to ride.

"Enough!" Prosper bellowed. When silence reigned and everyone looked at him again, he said at a more reasonable volume, "I'm of a good mind to shoot each and every one of you damn fools. I'd rather not do that. However, if any of you give me more trouble, I'll begin doing so, starting with him." Prosper pointed at one of the warriors and waited.

Finally, Iron Sky's shoulders slumped, and he nodded. As the changes were being made, Prosper asked the young woman, "You speak English, girl?"

"Little."

"What's your name?"

"Smoke Rising," she responded in a voice barely above a whisper.

Soon all was ready. One of the older women even picked up the bags of supplies and hung them over the back of the extra horse. Concerned the Ute woman might do something to hurt the baby, Prosper kept the basket hanging from his saddle horn. Lastly, Prosper placed a loop of rope around Iron Sky's neck. He looked at the other warriors. "Any of your men come after me on the trail, and Iron Sky will go under, whether you get me or not. Understand?"

There were a couple of terse nods, and then one warrior said, "You hurt Iron Sky, I kill you."

"You boys leave me be, he'll not be harmed. Now, go on, all of you, back to your village." He watched as the surly group trailed out of the boulders. A few minutes later, Prosper's small group did the same in the opposite direction.

CHAPTER 2

Prosper was tense as he rode along. While he really didn't expect the Utes to follow him and attack, he had to be alert to the possibility. In a way, he was glad of the Indians' superstition about this. It might make them keep their distance if they thought the baby cursed, and by extension, that he was a bad spirit. It slowly dawned on him that he might have doomed Smoke Rising. Her contact with the infant might have condemned her to be an outcast for the rest of her life. He regretted that, but there was little that could be done about it now. He would have to figure out something sooner or later, but he had other concerns that took priority. First among them was finding a home for Solo.

The group was silent as the people slowly made their way across the rocky landscape and through grassy meadows edged by stands of white aspens. The littlest member started squawking several miles down the trail. Prosper automatically reached for the small pouch of sugar, then stopped and dismounted.

"Time for you to do your duty, Smoke Rising," he said. He gave the basket containing Solo to the Ute woman, then remounted and moved on.

Smoke Rising took the basket and hung it from the horn of the white man's style saddle on her horse, then reached in and took the infant out. Her face was a ghastly mask of fear as if she would be struck dead by lightning if she brought the infant to her breast. She seemed surprised when nothing happened other than the baby latching onto her nipple and happily sucking. By the time they had gone another mile, Smoke Rising had relaxed.

With afternoon quickly fading, Prosper pushed them a little harder, aiming to reach the spot where he had camped the night before. They made it to the rocky tree-lined stream leading into the lake. There was little light left to the day but enough to get their chores done. As he dismounted, Prosper said, "Chief, you'll help me tend the horses. Smoke Rising, you..."

She was already off her pony and had set Solo down in his basket. She'd also taken the cradleboard off her back and set it next to the basket and was gathering firewood. Prosper nodded. By the time he and Iron Sky had taken care of the horses, Smoke Rising had a fire going and some elk stew heating in an iron pot. A coffee pot was set in the flames.

Before long, they were eating the simple but tasty meal. With a cup of coffee in hand after eating, Prosper stretched his legs out, thinking. He wondered if he could trust either of the Utes, but as he glanced from one to the other, that concern disappeared. Iron Sky was too worn out and possibly still too frightened of the bad spirit Prosper represented to cause any trouble. Smoke Rising seemed far less concerned about what might be a cursed child. She wasn't fussing over the boy. Indeed, she was almost ignoring him, but she did keep a watchful eye on the infant.

What occupied his mind far more was trying to figure out what to do with Solo. As a bounty hunter, he had few friends and no family, really, not close enough to approach with the task of raising a full-blooded Ute child. He couldn't just leave the infant at an orphanage. This was turning into more of a problem than he had figured on, not that he would have done any different. He could not have left this child out there to die, but finding him a home was looking like an almost unsolvable problem.

He finished his coffee, which had gone cold and sour, and tossed out the dregs. "Best get some sleep, you two. We got a lot of travelin' to do tomorrow," he said. As he closed his eyes, however, he muttered, "Hell if I know where, though."

By the time they pulled out, Prosper had decided that his only choice was to drop the boy off at a mission. He figured there should be any number of them in the New Mexico Territory. Likely Santa Fe, perhaps, or Albuquerque, so he headed southeast around and then away from the lake.

Two days later, Prosper decided he was safe enough from the Utes. That morning as they prepared to leave, Prosper told Iron Sky, "It's time you went back to your people, Chief."

"I go?" the old man questioned, eagerness in

his voice.

"You go." Prosper tossed him a knife and a tomahawk he had taken from the warriors at the start. "Those'll have to do for you."

"It okay." The older man grabbed them, stuck them in his belt, climbed on his horse, and left without looking back.

Smoke Rising watched him go. Prosper could see that she was both relieved and worried.

As he rode along, Prosper gave more thought to what to do with Solo. The more he considered it, the less he liked the idea of leaving the infant at a mission. The people there would likely destroy the boy's Ute-ness before he could even develop any. He finally put the puzzle out of his mind with great effort, so he was considerably surprised when about a quarter of an hour later, a possible solution popped into his mind. "Damn fool," he muttered. "Should've thought of it right off."

He was still pondering that a short while later when he caught a movement to his right, but it was not soon enough to get out of the way when a man launched himself off a boulder and slammed into him. Prosper landed in the dirt, and the man's momentum pushed him in a roll over Prosper. He came up with a knife in his hand. Prosper scrambled up as the man—a Ute, he presumed—rushed at him with the knife raised high, swinging toward Prosper.

The bounty hunter slammed a forearm into the warrior's arm, knocking the blade free, then swung around and pounded a fist into the Indian's jaw, sending him sprawling. Not knowing if there were other Utes in the area, Prosper pulled out his Starr, thumbing back the hammer as he did.

"No!" Smoke Rising screamed. She threw herself off her pony and ran to get between Prosper and the Indian, facing the former. Her face was pale with fear, and she was trembling.

"I told Iron Sky I'd kill anyone he sent against me," Prosper snarled. His blood was running high, as it always did in the midst of battle, and he was having trouble controlling himself. He still didn't know if other warriors were nearby, and he was not about to let this young man have another try at killing him.

Smoke Rising glanced over her shoulder. The young warrior lay on the ground, a little woozy. She said something to him in their language, and he briefly responded in a clipped voice.

"Iron Sky not send him," Smoke Rising said, looking at Prosper. "He come alone."

"I don't believe him."

"It true."

"How can I be certain?" Prosper was suspicious and wary but was settling down.

"He... We..."

Prosper looked beyond Smoke Rising at the man behind her. The young warrior had finally managed to get to his feet, though he was groggy. Prosper thought he saw something in the warrior's eyes and felt the same when he glanced at Smoke Rising. He uncocked the Starr and slid it back into the holster. "I believe it's time we had a talk. Smoke Rising, go loosen the saddles a bit so the horses can breathe. You," he added, nodding at the warrior and then pointing, "go sit over there. It's only by Smoke Rising's graces that you ain't dead, boy. She won't be able to stop me if you come at me again."

The two men stared at each other, then the Ute dropped his gaze and nodded. He sat where he was told to. Prosper picked up the Ute's knife and stuck it into his gun belt, then took a seat on a mostly flat rock. "You speak English, boy?"

"Speak good English." The surliness in his voice was unmistakable.

"Good. What's your name?"

"Painted Bear."

"I'm Elias."

A few minutes later, Smoke Rising was ready to join them. She stood, confused, worried, and seemingly eager to sit with Painted Bear but uncertain.

Prosper noticed her hesitancy and was even more certain now that there was something between the two Utes. He nodded in Painted Bear's direction. "Go ahead."

With some relief, Smoke Rising sat on Painted Bear's right, the basket with Solo on the ground to her right.

"All right, Painted Bear, if you weren't trailin' me because Iron Sky—or anyone else, you say— told you to, why were you doing so?" Silence hung in the air for a minute before Prosper sighed in exasperation, then voiced his suspicion, "Are you Smoke Rising's husband?"

"No," Painted Bear said in a voice that to Prosper was angry but also held sadness.

"You want to be, though, don't you?"

"Yes." Now he was defiant.

"So why ain't you?"

Painted Bear looked as if he were about to retort angrily, but Smoke Rising spoke to him in Ute, quietly and with obvious love in her voice and demeanor.

The warrior resisted for a minute or two, then breathed in deeply and let it out slowly. He looked over at Smoke Rising, and she nodded. He said something to her in Ute, and she nodded again after a moment's hesitation. Then she turned to look at Prosper.

"I seventeen summers," she said in her halting, accented English. "I had son eight moons ago." Tears filled her eyes. "He die..." Sobs overwhelmed her, and she had to stop speaking. She sat, shoulders shaking, breath coming in short, choking gasps.

Painted Bear self-consciously wrapped an arm around her and pulled her close to him. As she cried into his buckskin shirt, he said, "Boy die three, no, four moons ago. Boy's father"—he could not bring himself to say that man's name—"throw Smoke Rising away. Say she to blame, so he no want her anymore."

"Son of a bitch," Prosper murmured.

Painted Bear cracked the barest hint of a smile. "White-eyes have many good words for a man like that."

"So you married Smoke Rising?"

"No," the Ute warrior said, then added defiantly, "Not yet."

"I don't understand."

"Tell all," Smoke Rising muttered into Painted Bear's shirt.

As he talked, Painted Bear alternated between anger, shame, and defiance. "I wanted to marry Smoke Rising before. I played the flute for her..." He looked confused.

"Courted her," Prosper said.

"Yes. But her father, he like the other one better. Say I too young. Not yet as big a warrior. Don't have enough horses. The other, he richer than me, bigger warrior, more man." Painted Bear spat the last.

"You feel the same about Painted Bear, Smoke Rising?"

"Yes." There was no doubt, no shame in her response.

"So her pa made Smoke Rising marry that no good son of a bitch, eh?"

Both Utes answered yes in the same breath.

"Did you still court her after she married?"

"No. That wrong."

"Seems like you're an honorable man, Painted Bear."

The warrior shrugged. "I watch her, though. I hope. I think maybe she can get away, or he get tired of her. Once, twice, I talk to Smoke Rising. She feel the same, but she can't get free. He do it to make her and me sad. And father would be shamed. Then she has baby."

"Hurt you, didn't it?" Prosper asked quietly, a fleeting remembrance racing across his mind.

"Much. Then baby die." His lower lip trembled,

and he fought to hold back tears. Smoke Rising did not fight hers.

"So when that weasel left, you thought Smoke Rising'd be yours."

"Yes. But father say no. Man might come back."

"You think he will?"

Again both Utes answered in unison. "No."

"Then I come along, and her pa gives her over to me."

"Yes," Painted Bear snapped. "You gonna take her for yours. I kill you, take Smoke Rising back."

"I ain't aimin' to keep her. I ain't even gonna use her for myself. I just brought her along to care for the baby. Soon's I find a home for the child, Smoke Rising can go back to your people."

"You lie."

"No," Smoke Rising said quickly. "He no touch. Always kind. I just care for baby. Not share robes."

Painted Bear looked dubious but said, "Well, I take Smoke Rising and baby and go."

"Ain't you afraid that the boy's cursed?"

For a moment, fear flitted across Painted Bear's dark eyes. And, Prosper noticed, determination flickered in Smoke Rising's. She had become attached to the boy in the few days they had been together. Prosper had wondered about it, but now that he had heard the story, he was certain this orphaned infant had replaced her lost son in her heart. She was not going to let Painted Bear's doubts deter her from keeping the child.

Painted Bear shook himself as if ridding himself of spirits. "No. Foolish thoughts by the People."

Prosper nodded. "So, where're you plannin' to go with Smoke Rising and the baby? You gonna go back to the village?"

Smoke Rising gasped. "No!"

"Another Ute village?"

"No," Painted Bear conceded gruffly.

"Live on your own out here all by yourselves?"

The warrior looked as if he were about to reply in the affirmative until he saw the look in Smoke Rising's eye. "No," he grumbled.

Both Utes looked crestfallen.

CHAPTER 3

"I think maybe I got a solution," Prosper said. Both Utes perked up a little. "You mind hard work, Painted Bear? White man's hard work?"

"Never done. Won't farm, though."

Prosper grinned. "Me neither. I got a friend down near the Huerfano River. John's a good fella. I'm certain he'll take all of you in. You'd have to work, though."

"Do what?"

"Whatever he needs you to do. Carpentry, maybe blacksmithin', freightin'." He shrugged.

"I never did those things."

"You could learn.

Painted Bear looked unconvinced. "What about Smoke Rising?"

"She can help his wife with the other children, maybe with the garden, do some cookin'."

As Smoke Rising brought the infant to her breast, Painted Bear considered what Prosper had said for a few minutes. Then he shook his head.

"White man won't want some Utes livin' with him. Too much trouble. He and any others around, they'll treat us bad."

"Nope. Like I said, John's a good fella. Besides, he's a half-breed. His pa was a mountain man back many years ago. Married him a Shoshone woman. John's married to a native woman too. An Arapaho." Seeing the horror on the Utes' faces, he laughed. "I'm joshin'. Matilda is a Jicarilla. I understand your people are friendly with them. She'll be happy to take in three Utes."

Painted Bear looked confused until Smoke Rising jabbed him with an elbow and nodded at the infant at her breast. "Oh," he said sheepishly.

"So, what do you two think?"

"Is good," Smoke Rising said right away.

Painted Bear, however, was having doubts. "We have to become like white men. We no more be Nunt'zi."

"Reckon that's mostly true. But you'll be alive, and you can keep some of your ways. You can teach 'em to little Solo..." He stopped at their looks of confusion, and he smiled. "It's what I been calling the young'un. It means 'the only one.'"

"He not alone now," Smoke Rising said adamantly. "I call him..." She paused. "Yes, I will call him 'Lives Again.'"

"Sounds right reasonable to me." He asked, "So, Painted Bear, what do you say?"

Seeing Painted Bear's continued hesitation, he said, "I take no pleasure in what I'm about to say, Painted Bear, but it's gotta be said. Time's running out for the Utes. For all the nations. Many of the tribes are already on reservations, and those that ain't will be so in the next ten, twenty winters. Even some of the Utes, I've heard, are on reservations."

Painted Bear's face darkened and he started to protest, but Prosper held up a hand, stopping him. "It ain't right. I know that. But that won't stop it. There's too many whites, and they won't stop comin' and takin' your land. I wish whites and Indians could live together in peace, but wishin' won't change it."

Painted Bear had grown sullen, his face stony.

Smoke Rising broke the silence. "We go with you, Elias. Me and Lives Again. If Painted Bear not want to, we go anyway."

Painted Bear snapped something in Ute, and Smoke Rising responded in kind. The warrior sat, angry, bitter, defiant. Then his shoulders slumped. Gritting his teeth, he nodded.

"It'll be all right. You got Smoke Rising and Lives Again. A good family ready to take on the world. John and Matilda'll take good care of you and won't try to change you too much."

The warrior said nothing, just stared at the ground.

"You got a horse, I reckon?" Prosper said.

"Back in the rocks."

"Weapons with it?"

"Bow, a few arrows."

"Why didn't you just shoot me?"

"Wanted to kill you close. Not shoot from far away."

"Shows you're a brave warrior. Maybe foolish, though. Still, this way, we've been able to work things out. Now, go on and get your pony. Leave the bow on it."

Prosper waited, leaning against a rock, looking toward where the sounds of Painted Bear's movements came from. He had a pistol in hand, cocked. He uncocked it when Painted Bear came out of the brush, walking his horse. His bow and quiver were hanging from the front of his high-bow saddle.

The warrior looked at Prosper in annoyance, which bothered Prosper not a whit.

They were soon on their way. Still not sure he could trust Painted Bear, Prosper made the warrior take the lead. Smoke Rising came next, with Lives Again now in the cradleboard the woman had brought with her and towing the extra horse, and Prosper brought up the rear.

** ** ** ** **

"What does your friend do?" Painted Bear asked the next night when they were finishing their meal.

"Some farming, some ranching. Helps out people nearby who need blacksmithing or need a farrier..."

"What is farrier?"

"Fella who shoes horses."

"Seems foolish. Indian ponies aren't shoed. They do fine."

"Reckon so. Can't recall any Indian I saw—and I haven't seen that many—having a shod horse." He grinned a little. "Unless he stole a white man's horse."

"My people never do such things," Painted Bear said, then laughed.

Prosper laughed too. "John also helps folks in the

area with freighting—hauling things in a wagon. Helps out travelers on the trail from Taos to Pueblo. He butchers hogs and cattle. Does so with buffalo, too, but there aren't as many as there used to be."

"White men kill 'em for the hides," Painted Bear growled. "Take only them and maybe tongues. Leave rest to rot." His anger grew, and he looked at Prosper as if he were to blame and should be killed for it.

"Ain't my doin', amigo," Prosper said. "I shot a few of 'em before the war when I spent a short time with John and Matilda, but we gave most of the meat to Matilda's people." He paused. "How many buffalo have you killed?"

"Plenty, but they are our buffalo, not white man's."

"There's some who'd argue that with you." He grinned. "But I ain't one of them."

"Good thing," the Ute warrior grumbled.

"When the buffalo are gone—and that won't be many more years, I reckon—your people will be hard-pressed to feed and clothe themselves."

"I know," Painted Bear said, his voice containing a mixture of anger and sadness.

"Another good reason for you to stay with the Higginses."

"Where is this fella?"

"Like I said, he has a place along the Huerfano, a tributary of the Arkansas here in Colorado Territory."

"More land taken from my people." The Ute's bitterness had not lessened.

"More like the Cheyenne, from what I hear."

"My people."

"We'll be spending a lot of time on the trail together—the Huerfano's a couple weeks' ride, maybe more—and we can't keep arguing like this. I ain't responsible for what other white men have done to you or to your people any more than you're responsible for what's happened to the Shoshone or any other tribe. So quit your grousing about all the bad things the white man's done to your people. It'll make it a heap easier for our travel."

Painted Bear just grunted in response and left to go to his robes. Smoke Rising joined him.

Seeing that, as he had the previous couple of nights, made him wish Painted Bear hadn't come along. Not that he wanted Smoke Rising for himself, though she was a beautiful and desirable woman, but the two Utes' closeness and the sound of their lovemaking bothered him. It brought back memories both good and bad and made it difficult to get to sleep.

** ** ** ** **

"Time for you to do some huntin', Painted Bear," Prosper said in the morning. "I expect you can find us an elk or deer or something."

"I can," the Ute said arrogantly.

"Just make sure you don't try huntin' me." Prosper didn't like the look Painted Bear gave him, but the bounty hunter relaxed when Smoke Rising said something to her man in Ute.

Painted Bear still looked angry. He finished his coffee and tossed his cup in the dirt as he rose.

"We'll be heading southeast like we have been,"

Prosper said.

Painted Bear grunted in response and went to his horse.

Prosper watched him for a few moments, wondering if he had made a mistake. He was not sure he could trust Painted Bear.

"You be all right," Smoke Rising said. "He won't hurt you."

"You certain?"

"Yes. I tell him if he hurt you, I leave him."

Prosper laughed. "Ain't nowhere you can go if you leave him."

Smoke Rising turned her bright eyes on Prosper. "He know, I know, but not matter. I not have to leave. Ignore him."

"He won't force you?"

"Maybe, maybe not. But no joy for him."

"Sure hope it doesn't come to that, for my sake as well as yours." He pushed himself up. "Well, we best get on the trail." He headed off to saddle the horses.

Prosper rode with shoulders hunched, waiting for an arrow to strike him despite Smoke Rising's assurances.

Painted Bear rode up just after noon, a deer carcass tied on the back of the extra horse.

"Looks like you did well, Bear."

The compliment earned another grumpy grunt from the Ute.

"Go on up ahead," Prosper said, not bothering to hide the irritation in his voice.

They stopped a little early and enjoyed the fresh deer, which Painted Bear had butchered while

Prosper was tending the animals and Smoke Rising was caring for Lives Again and starting a fire.

Rain began before the two men had finished their chores, which did little to obviate all three's irritation. Smoke Rising had, however, gotten a good fire going in the partial shelter of a rock, and meat was roasting and coffee heating. Prosper pulled on his loose-fitting frock coat against the weather. Not having extra protection from the weather did not seem to bother the two Utes.

With a long way yet to travel, Prosper got them back on the trail early the next morning, even though the rain continued and at times increased. The wind picked up, broken only by the thick stands of aspens and pines. The ground became muddy, and whatever rocky spots they traveled were slippery.

Prosper called an early stop again, and the three adults grumbled at the weather as they threw up their camp. It was a familiar routine now and did not take long. After eating, Painted Bear hastily built a ramshackle lean-to for him, Smoke Rising, and the infant. Prosper decided not to bother. When the time for sleep came, he simply spread out his bedroll under a tall spruce, which did a fair job of protecting him from the rain. After a last pipe, he laid down and was asleep in minutes.

The new day broke with an abundance of sunshine, which sparked their cheerfulness, and it was with brighter dispositions that they pulled out.

CHAPTER 4

"What were you doing when you found baby?" Painted Bear asked a few nights later as they sat around the fire, enjoying the meat of the elk the Ute had killed that afternoon.

Prosper thought the young Ute might actually be interested, which surprised him. "Heading toward Texas."

"Where from?"

"Up northwest, from near a place where a big lake, a salty one, gives the town Salt Lake City its name."

"What you do before that?"

"Handled some business out in a place called California."

"Where is that?"

Prosper pointed west. "A far piece from here. More than twenty suns, along a great ocean."

"What is 'ocean'?"

"You know that big lake I just mentioned?" When Painted Bear nodded, he said, "Well, if you take as many lakes as there are buffalo and add a lot more, that'd be the Pacific Ocean."

"I don't believe."

Prosper shrugged. "Don't matter none to me if you do or not. It's a fact"

"Why you in this strange-sounding place?

"Had some business to tend to."

"What business?"

"None of your concern, boy," Prosper snapped.

"You run from war, then come back when it all over?" Painted Bear asked with a sneer.

"Had my fill of that war in the middle of it. Stuck with it 'til my enlistment was up after a few years, then turned to other things."

"What you do?"

"I tried bartendin' for a spell, but I didn't take to it much. Then I apprenticed to a gunsmith, but I realized pretty soon that I was better at using guns than repairing 'em."

"What you do now?"

Prosper decided there was no reason not to answer. "Round up bad guys and bring 'em to justice."

"Catch 'em or kill 'em?"

"It's up to them. They come along peaceable, that's best. They want to make a fight of it, they'll lose."

"Sure of yourself, eh?"

"I'm still here. Those others aren't."

"Maybe you are warrior. But you must face a real warrior alone to prove it."

"Soon's I find a real warrior, I just might challenge him," Prosper said dryly.

Painted Bear scowled, stood, and stalked away. Hiding her face from him, Smoke Rising smiled a little.

"You best be mindful of him, Smoke. He's a hothead and will likely cause trouble sooner rather than later. Hate to see you and the baby hurt because he can't control his temper."

"He a good man."

"I don't doubt it, but good men can be troublemakers too, and that can lead to danger for others who aren't deserving of such treatment as they hand out."

"I be careful." Smoke Rising took another small piece of meat and put most of it into her mouth. She took the tiny piece that was left and gave it to Lives Again to let him gum it for a while. Then she asked, "What this place called Calif..."

"California."

"Yes. What it like?"

"Depends on where you are there. It's a mighty big place, bigger even than the land you had before the government took much of it away." He shook his head in annoyance, realizing he should not have said that last part. However, it was too late now, so he just plunged ahead. "In the south, it's powerful nice. Warm but not too warm all the year 'round. Nice breeze comin' off the ocean. Many Mexicans. I've heard they used to be welcoming many years ago, but they've been facin' the same troubles as the Utes for many years. I hear they ain't so friendly to the whites these days, but they're outnumbered, with more settlers comin' every day." He took a few moments to sip some coffee.

"But when you get into the mountains—the Sierra

Nevada, they're called—the weather is much harsher. Tough passes to get through. Sometimes snow gets to be as deep as one pony on top of another."

"You fool me."

"Nope. It's all true. Seen it with my own eyes once."

"Why anyone go to place like that and not where weather is nice?"

Prosper glanced up as Painted Bear returned. "Gold, at first. Some just stayed in the places where gold had been a long time ago. Others got partway across and decided to stay where they were." He grinned. "Of course, most of 'em were dumb as ducks."

Smoke Rising laughed.

"There's a big stretch of valley between those mountains and others along the coast. Very good for growing crops."

"Utes grow small things. No good, stay one place to farm." She grimaced.

"Hate to say it, but you won't have much choice before too many years pass." Seeing the sudden sadness on the girl's face, he added, "Maybe you'll change your mind when you get to John and Matilda's and you see how they can farm yet still keep some of the old ways. And still do some huntin'." He grinned. "Well, Painted Bear will do the huntin'."

Smoke Rising brightened a little. Having heard the talk of California, Painted Bear had returned and took his seat.

"It'll be harder on Painted Bear. Huntin' will be less frequent, and he won't be able to just ride around where he pleases."

"Why not?" the warrior asked.

"The way it's going, I don't think many whites will feel comfortable with a warrior ridin' around loose. There'll be trouble like as not."

"Won't be me causin' it."

"You sure about that? Some feller sees you on his ranchland, he'll figure you're out to shoot some of his cattle. If he can, he'll shoot you. If he can't, he'll huddle with his family until you're gone, then get a posse or vigilance group to chase you down."

"They not catch me."

"Yeah, they will, Painted Bear. They'll hire some old mountain man or a half-breed, or hell, one of your own tribe to chase you down."

"I'll go far," the Ute insisted.

"Unless you can make it to Canada and find a home there, you'll be hunted down. May take a while, but they'll get you."

"Bah!" Painted Bear snapped. "I beat them all."

"Like hell, you will." Seeing Painted Bear's continued intransigence, Prosper said, "Look, boy, I ain't sayin' this to annoy you or belittle you. Just telling the truth as I see it. Your world and your way of life are coming to an end, and that loss will come in your lifetime. Best prepare for it so's you can do what's necessary."

** ** ** ** **

Painted Bear was sullen as he rode for the next few days. Several times Prosper nearly approached the young warrior to talk to him. But Smoke Rising stopped him each time after Painted Bear had stalked off for one reason or another.

"Painted Bear is proud warrior," she said one day while Painted Bear was off hunting. "He angry how people treat him when he want to marry me, even after...after I lose..."

Prosper laid a large work-hardened hand on her shoulder. "No need to relive that, Smoke."

Smoke Rising was able to hold back the tears that were forming. She cleared her throat, then continued. "He good man but stubborn and foolish. But he care for me and the baby, I think."

"Still, if he doesn't control his temper, he'll come to a bad end and soon. That'll leave you and Lives Again with no one to care for you." Prosper smiled. "Except John and Matilda Higgins and whoever else they have around their place. There's usually a heap of people around there. A real mix, too: Jicarillas, maybe some Utes, Mexicans, half-breeds, old trappers, whites, some official, some not, bullwhackers, sometimes travelers."

"Bullwhackers?"

"Folks who drive wagons of goods. The wagons are usually pulled by oxen—big cows, though not as sturdy as buffalo. A bullwhacker drives 'em along by snapping a whip at 'em."

"Oh." She grinned. "White man have strange ways."

"Same could be said about your people. There are times when that's a bad thing. Sometimes, though, it can be interestin'."

Smoke Rising nodded and quieted a fussing Lives Again. Then she asked, "The people—all different kinds—there all the time?"

"Some of 'em live in houses nearby. Others drift in and out. One day you might see fifty people there, the next just a couple dozen—twenty or so. It's a good place. John and Matilda are right fine folks, joyful most often, hard-working, trustful, benevolent."

"What does last thing mean?"

"Benevolent?" When she nodded, he said, "Being kind to folks, helping out when they can, not asking for anything in return."

"Some of my people like that."

"I reckon they are. It's nice to come across people you can put your trust in, ones you don't have to worry about making a sneak attack on your camp."

"Yes, is very good. I think I like the people where you take us. If they nice, I tell 'em you mean to me and Lives Again." She began to giggle. "Starve us, and we walk until we almost there. You..." She had to stop since she was running out of breath as she laughed.

"They'll likely believe you too." Prosper laughed as well. "But I'll get mean and nasty because of it and make you work putting bales of hay in the loft and loadin' and unloadin' wagons. And I'll make Lives Again help you!"

Both roared with laughter.

"What're you laughin' at?" Painted Bear demanded, having returned. He was no jollier than he had been when he stalked off.

"Makin' fun of you," Prosper said. He had stopped laughing, but he was still grinning. "I was tellin' Smoke Rising that your feet are too small for a feller who fancies himself a big man, and I think your eyes are crooked." He started to laugh again but stopped, worried now. Painted Bear's stare shifted between Prosper and Smoke Rising, and Prosper could see the danger to the woman in his eyes.

"Oh, hell, we were doing no such thing, Bear," Prosper said. "Now sit down, have some more food, and stop being such a frumptious snot. You ain't scarin' nobody here except maybe Lives Again, and he won't fight you. Yet." There was a small smirk on Prosper's face.

The Ute plopped down, cut off a piece of elk meat, and gnawed angrily.

"You know, boy, life'd go a heap easier for you if you were to stop being a cranky young botheration. There's no need to act like you have been. You got a good woman and now a child to help look after. He needs to be taught the ways of the Ute, the ways of being a man, though you certainly need some practice at the last there. You got many years ahead of you, boy. Well, maybe not, considerin' the way you act too often."

He paused for a sip of coffee, then continued. "No one here thinks you're a coward. It took a heap of courage to come chasin' after me and Smoke Rising. It took a man to accept a child that wasn't his. You're doin' all right, boy, some of the time. Do that more often, and nobody'll call you less than a man." He grinned. "And if he does, he'll not live through it."

He paused again. "Now, me and Smoke were just havin' some laughs about what it might be like livin' with Higginses and all the others who drift in and out of their place. It'd be good for you, too, to have a few laughs now and again. Just might crack that stone face of yours, 'Course, it just might fall off at such a strange thing." He smiled.

Across the fire, Smoke Rising tried unsuccessfully to hold in a giggle as Painted Bear stomped away again.

CHAPTER 5

The first arrow caught Prosper in the side as he bent over near the fire while reaching for a cup of coffee. The second got him in the leg as he tumbled over and landed in the flames. He managed to jump up with no damage from the fire, but the arrows might be a different matter. However, the angle of the first arrow's entrance had kept the bolt from entering too deeply, and the position of his leg had left the arrow barely sticking in the limb.

"You son of a bitch, Painted Bear!" Prosper shouted as he ducked behind a rock and tore out the arrows.

"Not Painted Bear!" Smoke Rising yelled as she jumped up and headed for where the baby hung from a tree limb in his cradleboard.

"Like hell."

He quickly checked his wounds. They were not bad, he decided.

He ran after Smoke Rising and the infant. With one strong hand, he grabbed the woman by the collar of her buckskin dress and yanked her around the tree just as another arrow thudded into the trunk.

"You sure that ain't Painted Bear?" Prosper asked.

She peeked around the tree to look at the arrow. "Is not him," she said firmly. "Different arrow."

"I'll believe it when I wring that little bastard's neck.

"He not shoot you." Smoke Rising insisted, but she sounded nervous and frightened.

"We'll see." He looked around, worried though not desperate. Yet. He spotted a thick stand of currant bushes. "Make your way into that thicket there with the baby," he said urgently, pointing.

The Ute woman nodded and began burrowing into the thickly growing bushes.

He glanced around again, wondering if Painted Bear was alone or if he had somehow connected with some fellow warriors, maybe one day while he was supposedly hunting. Prosper wished he had his Henry rifle, which was leaning against his saddle a few yards away Then he realized it would not be all that effective among the trees. He pulled his Starr and began to move to his right, deeper into the trees and rocks, uneasy because he knew he was no match for Painted Bear or any other Indian in the woods like this.

Suddenly a warrior popped up in front of him, knife in hand, ready to attack. Through sheer luck, Prosper managed to ward off the blow and fire his pistol, blowing a hole through the man's innards. The warrior fell, and Prosper breathed a sigh of relief. He was also glad to see the one he had just killed was not Painted Bear. It didn't mean Painted Bear hadn't somehow called in help, though.

A war cry to his right came from a warrior rushing at him, tomahawk raised. He was so close, Prosper didn't even have time to bring his pistol to bear on the man. He only just managed to block the Indian's tomahawk arm. The warrior crashed into him, jarring his pistol loose. Prosper shoved him away, then rammed his shoulder into his foe's stomach. He lifted the man, surged forward a few steps, and slammed the warrior into the wide trunk of a sturdy spruce but not before he had received a weak clout across his back from the tomahawk. The Indian sagged, and Prosper let him fall in a heap.

Another warrior burst out from behind a boulder. He also had a tomahawk ready to split Prosper's head. The white man dove, rolled, came up with his Starr in hand, and fired twice within a second. Both lead balls hit the charging warrior in the chest but did not stop the man's momentum. The warrior ran into Prosper, though without much force, and sliced a thin, shallow groove in Prosper's forearm before he fell to the ground where his blood puddled under him.

Prosper reloaded the pistol and slid it back into his holster. He was thankful that the trees were packed as tightly as they were since it meant the warriors could not use their bows. Had they been able to do so, he would have been dead several times over by now.

Suddenly he heard horses racing away. He stepped up to the edge of the glade where he and the others had camped and spotted at least two warriors riding hellbent for leather down what passed for a trail. He ran for his Henry, but it was too late; the Indians were out of sight amid the trees.

"You all right, Smoke? You and the baby?"

"Yes," came the faint reply.

"Best stay there a while longer."

"No," Smoke Rising said as she clambered out of her makeshift foliage fort, still clutching Lives Again. She came up to stand at his side.

'Why ain't you listenin' to me, girl? It might not be safe."

"We fine. I make sure you not shoot Painted Bear."

"That'll take some doing, girl," Prosper said sharply. "I don't fancy being attacked by a bunch of Indians of any kind, let alone a bunch of Utes trying to help one of their own while I'm trying to help three of 'em."

"But they not..."

Painted Bear walked jubilantly out of the forest across the glade from Prosper and Smoke Rising.

"Stop right there, boy, and drop the bow!"

Prosper could see the Ute's frown across the small glade and a kernel of doubt crossed his mind. "Do it!"

An angry Painted Bear considered the command for a moment, then decided he was no match with his bow and arrow against Prosper's pistol. The white man held it in hand, though not pointed directly at him.

"I told you what'd happen if you went against me, Painted Bear. I don't know how you got ahold of these other boys here, but it doesn't sit right with me."

"They not Utes," Smoke Rising insisted.

"Listen to her, white-eye," Painted Bear snapped.

Suddenly doubtful, Prosper glanced down at Smoke Rising. "If they ain't Utes, what are they?"

"Arapaho. Can tell by dress and hair and markings on arrows."

"You sure? You ain't tryin' to fool me?"

"No. I not do that. You take care of me and Lives Again."

"I'd like to believe you, Smoke, but I don't know that I can trust Painted Bear. He and I ain't on the best of terms."

Painted Bear heard him. "If I wanted to kill you, white-eye, you would've been dead the first time you sent me out huntin'."

His anger was growing, Prosper could see. "Maybe you were just waitin' on some others to make sure you didn't get shot while you were tryin' to kill me."

"You're touched, white-eye."

"Maybe I am, which if I understand you people means I'm safe around you because you and most other Indians think someone who's touched is bad medicine or some such nonsense."

Smoke Rising tugged on Prosper's sleeve, and he looked down at her. "Is true about Arapahos," she said, the pleading evident in her eyes. "I tell you. I not lie."

Prosper looked down into those soft brown eyes. It suddenly occurred to him that he loved her, though he did not know her all that well. He sighed. She did not love him, she loved Painted Bear. He decided on the spot that if he could not love her as a man should love a woman, he would love her as if he were her older brother. He was not all that happy about such a thing, but it was best for both of them. He would not tell her of his feelings, but he would know them in his heart.

"All right," he said quietly. "But you best talk to Painted Bear to make sure he doesn't try something against me. I still don't trust him, and he sure as hell doesn't trust me."

"I talk, he listen." She continued to gaze up at him. "I trust you?"

"As long as he doesn't come against me in any way, I'll not harm him."

"Good," she responded, and Prosper could hear the determination in her voice. "You hurt him, I kill you."

Prosper smiled, but he was serious when he said, "I do believe you would. Or at least try."

Smoke Rising broke off her gaze after a few more moments, then said something to Painted Bear in their language. He responded, anger written on his face. The confrontation continued for a bit before Painted Bear picked up his bow and headed back into the woods.

"What'd you say to him, Smoke? He didn't look very happy about it."

"I tell him if he hurt you, I hurt him. If not do that, I kill self. Maybe Lives Again. He not like that."

"I don't either." He reached down to feel his wounded side, and his hand came away bloody.

"You hurt!" Smoke Rising exclaimed.

"Ain't bad," he said calmly, though the wound had

begun to hurt enough that it might be worse than he'd thought. "Got a scratch on my leg and arm too. They ain't bad. I'll be all right."

"Side not bad, but I fix. Come to fire and sit."

** ** ** ** **

Prosper and Painted Bear were wary around each other afterward, each keeping a sharp eye on the other, half-expecting an attack. Prosper rode at the rear, Smoke Rising with Lives Again towing the extra horse between him and Painted Bear when the latter was not hunting. When they traveled in this formation, Prosper was sure Painted Bear was riding with hunched shoulders, waiting for a bullet in the back. When Painted Bear was hunting, Prosper worried that the young warrior would put an arrow in him from behind a tree.

Nights were not much better. The two men glowered at each other while performing their tasks or eating. Prosper slept lightly, as did Painted Bear, he suspected.

Smoke Rising put up with it for several days before she had had enough. One night after they had filled up on deer and had coffee, the two men growled at each other since each wanted the last of their sugar supply.

With a shake of her head, Smoke Rising stood. "Stop!" she shouted. "You like childs. Both. You," she pointed at Prosper, "worry when Painted Bear gone. You," her accusing finger shifted to stab the air at Painted Bear, "worry Elias shoot you."

"But..." Painted Bear interrupted first.

"Hush," Smoke Rising snapped. "I not finished. You stop foolishness. It dangerous. One kill other, only one left to take me and Lives Again to safety. Maybe Arapahos attack, kill me, steal Lives Again. Maybe bear get me and baby. Or wolves. You kill other, no one protect me and Lives Again. Nowhere to go. No food. I not have milk for baby. We die if you not like each other."

She cut Painted Bear off again when he tried to interject something in Ute. "You promise not act bad. Promise help each other. And me. You not, I not cook for you. Not help. Just care for Lives Again." She looked from one to the other, her face a mask of anger...and a little fear.

Prosper stared at her a few moments, then grinned. Looking at Painted Bear, he said, "She's a feisty one, ain't she?"

"What is 'feisty'?"

"Spirited."

"I say so too. We be friends," Painted Bear said. He smiled.

"Friends," Prosper said with a nod. Despite the smile on Painted Bear's face, Prosper did not like the look in the warrior's eyes. He would continue to be wary.

CHAPTER 6

An uneasy truce settled over the nightly camps. As they had all along, during the day Painted Bear did the hunting, Prosper set the direction and made sure they kept to it, and Smoke Rising cared for Lives Again. When they made camp, the warrior butchered the meat, Prosper cared for the animals, and the woman gathered firewood and got a fire going. Prosper usually ended up helping to gather wood and bucketing up water since Painted Bear would not do it.

One night Prosper had just dumped another load of wood by the fire when Painted Bear said with a sneer, "My woman has trained you well, white-eye."

"Hogwash," Prosper said tightly as he flopped down near the fire. "It's just that she could use a bit of help now and again, and I ain't afraid I'll lose my stones if I give her that help. Unlike some lazy no-account Ute I know of."

Painted Bear reached for the last hunk of meat hanging over the fire, but Prosper was faster, stabbing it with his knife and flinging it toward the Ute. It landed in the dirt next to his leg. "Eat hearty, friend," Prosper said, and this time it was he who wore the sneer.

Painted Bear started to get up, looking as if he were going to pull his knife and attack Prosper. But the latter drew his pistol. "Sit," he ordered. When the Ute had, Prosper put the Starr back into its holster. "You really got to learn to behave. Stop being all jumpy and such. I've promised Smoke Rising that I'd not harm you unless you came against me. I aim to keep that promise. I also aim to keep my hair. If I'm gonna break the promise, I might end up without the hair, but maybe not."

Painted Bear sat sullen and brooding.

"Look, boy, we said we'd be friends. You and I both know that's goat droppin's. But we can at least be civil to each other for the sake of Smoke Rising and Lives Again if nothing else."

This time Painted Bear expressed himself with a grunt, though Prosper did not know what it meant.

"I'm gettin' tired of all this tension 'tween us. It's wearin' on a body, and I ain't gonna put up with it much longer."

"What'll you do?" Painted Bear asked with a smirk.

"Kill you," Prosper said simply and quietly.

"Smoke Rising not like that." The Ute grinned insolently.

"She'd get over it. And she'd get a decent man— red or white—to marry her and care for her and Lives Again. Before long, you'd be a little more than an almost-remembered vision of the past. So, if you want to be a man, act like one. It won't take much trying on your part, though as hardheaded as you are, maybe it will."

Painted Bear said nothing, and the three people fell silent. The only sounds to be heard were the crackling of the fire, the shuffling of the horses, and the light wind soughing through the trees.

Finally Smoke Rising asked, "How you come here?"

"Told you, I had business in California." He was surprised.

The Ute looked embarrassed and tried again. "Where you come from?"

"I told..."

"No. Long time. When young."

"Oh, you want to know about my life?"

"Yes, yes. I listen, Lives Again listen. We learn about you, maybe learn ways of these people you takin' us to."

"I reckon it won't do you any good, and it'll bore you to tears, but I'll tell you some things." He lit a small pipe and poured himself a new cup of coffee.

"Me and my brothers and sisters—there was eight of us altogether—grew up in a place called Missouri."

"Do all whites have so many children?" Smoke Rising asked, amazed.

"Well, not all, of course, but many. Don't Indians?"

"No. We have two, maybe three."

It was Prosper's turn to be amazed. "Seems odd to me, but I reckon your people are different. But we were all happy, I suppose. My pa was a wheelwright. That's someone who makes wheels for wagons and such."

"Wagons to bring more people to steal our land," Painted Bear said angrily.

Prosper decided not to argue with the Ute. "Ma, of course, stayed home with us young'uns. Pa was successful, so we lived well. We weren't rich, mind you, but comfortable. Because of that, I got more schoolin' than most kids at that time."

"Another foolish white-eye thing," Painted Bear said. "Learnin' numbers and letters no good for anything."

"You and your people learned numbers and letters, you might not be taken advantage of in treaties and in tradin'."

"White-eyes lie in both. Don't matter we don't know those markings on paper."

Prosper shrugged. He could see no use in debating it. The Ute would never be convinced. "Things were fine 'til the war broke out, when people from the North fought those from the South. Me and two brothers joined the Northern side. Two other brothers went to the Southern side. It was that kind of war."

"Foolish," Smoke Rising said.

"True enough."

"Why you fight?"

"Something called slavery, when one person owns another like you own your horses. Whites owned blacks. Didn't seem right to me that one person should own another. Not that it made a big difference to me. My folks never owned slaves and had no intention of doing so. Mainly 'cause we didn't have the money to do so. "My two brothers who took the South's side differed in opinion on the matter." He shrugged.

"I was wounded at a place called Spotsylvania Court House in a state named Virginia, back in May of '64. Got our asses whupped pretty good there. Lost a heap of good men. So did the Confederacy, but not near as many as we did. I managed to get to a surgical hospital where they patched me up, and I spent a few months in the capital recuperatin'. By then, the South was on its heels and the war looked to be nearing an end, so I was released from the Army. I went back home, but things were no better with all the squabblin'. One of my brothers on the Northern side had been killed, and the other was lost. Everyone figured he was dead. Of the two fightin' for the South, one was killed. The other came home, too."

Prosper sighed, thinking back on it. "That made things twitchy around the farmstead, so I pulled up stakes and headed west, then south into Texas, just driftin' with no object in mind. By then the war was about over, and the North started what they called Reconstruction. I joined up with a Reconstruction outfit there, but I decided that running roughshod over men and families who had given their all for what they believed in, as wrong as I thought that might be, was not something I wanted to be doing. I had learned that men, former Rebs mostly, though some Yanks, too, were robbin' trains and stages and doing all types of deviltry. I headed to the Indian Territory," he grinned wryly at the reference, "where there was little law. I started chasing outlaws then, spending part of my time in the Indian Territory and the rest in Texas. That was more than a year ago. Been doing such ever since. Chased some bad men to California and spent the winter there."

"You like that?" Smoke Rising asked.

"Can't say as I like it, really. Can't say I don't, either. It's something to do, and I do it well. Maybe I'm a fool stayin' with it, but I can't think of anything else to do. I chase the worst of the outlaws. It's more dangerous, but the rewards are higher."

"Not quit?"

"Not 'til now," Prosper said with a laugh. "If I had known I was gonna be herdin' a couple of Utes—three if you count the baby and one of 'em a perpetual headache—I likely would have given up and stayed in California, maybe fishin' for a livin', though I hate fish."

Painted Bear glowered, but Smoke Rising smiled.

"So, how about you, Painted Bear?" Prosper asked. "You been on the warpath?"

"Two times. Counted coup three times, have two scalps."

"No, you got a few more. 'Course, you can't show 'em to your people, but at least you and I and Smoke Rising here know you to be a great warrior."

The Ute scowled some more.

"Hadn't stolen enough horses, though, did you? Not enough to pay Smoke Rising's bride price?"

"No!" Painted Bear spat.

"Well, don't go frettin' on it. There's no need now. You're here, she's here, and you're both going to a place where you can be free of having to prove yourself every day."

"I'd rather be with my people."

"You can do that. Just turn your ass around and head back. I ain't sure they'll take you in again, though, considerin' you've been travelin' with a cursed baby."

"Close mouth, white-eye."

Prosper grinned rather insolently. "Of course, Smoke Risin' wouldn't be going with you. Not unless she was to rid herself of that child, and she ain't about to do that. Not for you, me, or anybody else. You may not like it, but that infant is yours now, son. Best get used to it."

As he so often did, Painted Bear rose and stalked away, anger evident from his stiff back and the clenched fists at his sides.

Prosper laughed, then looked at Smoke Rising and winked. She smiled back.

Painted Bear was no more amiable the next morning or the one after that. Both days he gobbled down a hasty breakfast, saddled his mustang and rode out. He invariably came back with a half-butchered deer or elk, so the feeding was good for all of them.

During the evenings in camp, Prosper did not bother to try to make small talk with the Ute, only with Smoke Rising. He had grown even more protective of her as the days passed, and he was wary of Painted Bear. He did not trust the Ute warrior, even though he obviously considered Smoke Rising his wife. Still, Prosper had heard that Indian men didn't treat their women very well. He wasn't sure if that was true, but it seemed that he was treating her less pleasantly than when he had first joined them. He also seemed to be less accepting of Lives Again as time passed. Prosper began to wish he had never taken on this task. His destination was still a fair distance, and with tensions rising, trouble was bound to break out.

Two days later, Painted Bear left camp as usual in the morning, but he returned early, laden as always with meat. As he often did when he was with Prosper, Smoke Rising, and Lives Again, he took his place leading the small caravan.

Prosper was a bit surprised but said nothing.

Early in the afternoon, Painted Bear halted suddenly, holding up a hand to stop the others. Prosper pulled up alongside Smoke Rising, waiting nervously. A few moments later, the Ute jerked his horse's head around, kicked it into a lope, and dashed into the trees. "Run!" he yelled.

Prosper did not take the time to answer. He grabbed the rope rein of Smoke Rising's horse and yanked it with him as he darted into the forest. A small fusillade rang out, ripping through leaves and into trunks.

CHAPTER 7

"Come on out, redskins," someone yelled from behind the trees on the other side of a stream.

Even with the sound of lazily running water, Prosper and the others could hear the sniggers in the voice.

"You come out, white-eyes," Painted Bear shouted in return.

"Reckon not, boy."

"Bunch of soft white men, ain't you? Remind me of women in my village. Reckon you not show selves because you not want us to see you wearin' dresses."

"You ain't gonna be a man at all once we get done with you, boy." The voice held anger, not snickers this time.

Behind some brush, Prosper dismounted. His eyes searched the foliage across the stream, trying to find the body that belonged to the voice and see if there were others with him. He assumed the man was not alone and silently debated whether he should make himself known to the attackers. They might back off if they knew a white man was with the Indian they had seen. On the other hand, they might get more determined to kill Painted Bear and Prosper himself as an Indian lover. What they would do to Smoke Rising was something Prosper did not want to contemplate.

Prosper and Smoke Rising dismounted. He gave the reins of his horse to the Ute woman, who took them without a word. Then Prosper reached into his coat pocket and pulled out a small revolver. "You know how to use this?" he whispered. When she nodded, he gave it to her. Then he pulled his Henry from the saddle scabbard and started making his way toward where he had seen Painted Bear crouch in the vegetation.

"Put the 'hawk away, you stupid bastard," Prosper snapped in a whisper as he neared Painted Bear. The Ute had heard him coming and was waiting, tomahawk in hand.

"I keep it. I not sure you ain't with them over there."

"Now, how in hell could I be one of them when I been with you for the past week? You think I could've turned into an eagle, flew all the way here, retook my human form, told some pukin' white men where we'll be, turned back into an eagle, and flew back here and turned back into myself, all the while you not knowin' nothing of it?"

"White men have strange ways."

"You're even a bigger idiot than I thought." He paused. "You have any idea how many are over there?"

"Two. More maybe. One behind big hackberry bush, one behind cottonwood to right."

"You know this country any?"

"Some. Why?"

"There anyplace upstream or downstream not too far where I can cross over and maybe get behind them?"

Painted Bear didn't have to think long. "Upstream is waterfalls. No good to cross there. Downstream is good. Quarter-mile or little more so those devils there not see you."

Prosper nodded. Before he could say anything more, another short hail of bullets flew into the foliage, none of it near the two men or the woman.

"I reckon there's three at least. I saw smoke comin' from three places."

"I saw too."

"Think you can get a shot at 'em?"

"Can't waste arrows just to scare 'em. I shoot if any stick head into open."

"It's all I can expect. I don't think it's a good idea to be shooting at ghosts. Besides, you'd give your position away."

"I shoot, then move. Fast," Painted Bear said dryly.

Prosper nodded, not catching the sarcasm in the Ute's words. "Smoke Rising and Lives Again have moved deeper into the trees and brush, away from the trail," Prosper said. "She's got an extra pistol of mine in case she finds herself alone."

"Meaning you, me dead."

"Yup. And while I'm out there riskin' my neck to save your hide, I'd rather you didn't think of grabbin'

Smoke and haulin' your ass and hers down the trail back to your land. I'd think most unkindly of that."

Painted Bear shrugged. "I not care what you think."

"You will when I hunt you down and put a bullet in that thick head of yours. Now, pay attention to them boys over there." He slipped away.

Prosper estimated he had come roughly a quarter-mile, so he crossed the stream. It was not deep or running very fast, so it took little effort. He hated getting his boots wet, which made them uncomfortable, but crossing in his socks or bare feet would not be much better, he figured. Better to have boots, socks, and feet all get wet rather than just some of them.

He pushed east and deeper into the forest before turning north. He wished he was better at moving quietly through the woods, thinking he sounded like a moose romping in the wild. As he neared the place where he believed the enemy was, he tried harder to creep along. The stream's soft burbling helped cover the sounds he was making. He was thankful for that when he spotted a man lying behind a log, Henry resting on the wood.

Prosper crept up, his own Henry in hand. The man sensed someone behind him and turned his head just in time to catch a rifle butt on the forehead. His face fell in the dirt.

Prosper knelt lightly on the man's back to keep him down but not hard enough to injure him, then laid the Henry on the ground next to him. Prosper grabbed the rifleman's hair and pulled his head back. The man seemed groggy but aware. "I'm gonna ask you some questions, pard, and it'd behoove you to answer quickly and quietly.

The man snorted in derision. "What're you gonna do, shoot me? That'd bring others to gun you down. If I was you, I'd skedaddle and let us finish off that horse-thievin' redskin."

"He ain't a horse thief, and I don't need a pistol. I got this." Prosper pulled his thick, heavy Bowie and placed it gently against the man's exposed neck. "Why're you shooting at us?"

"Told ya. We been chasin' that damned redskin for a week after he stole a couple horses from us."

"That's mighty interestin', considerin' he's been with me for more than a week, and we're comin' from the west while you've been chasin' someone to the west. I don't know what you and your pals..."

"I'm alone."

"That's a load of manure as big as a house. You already said 'others.' As I was sayin', I don't know what you and your pals're doing out here, but I don't think you were chasin' a horse thief. I think you just saw an Indian and decided you wanted a trophy."

The man shrugged as well as he could in his position.

"Now, how many are there of you boys?"

"Hell with you."

"I do not have boundless supplies of patience. In fact, I'm damn near out of it already. Answer me."

"No need for me to do so."

"That so? What makes you think that?"

"You try torturin' me, and I'll get a least one scream out to alert the others. And if you kill me, you'll get no answers."

"You that ready to die to protect your pals?"

Once again, he shrugged as well as he could.

"Not really, but I don't think you got the stones to up and kill a man just layin' here."

"You're wrong." Prosper swiped the knife across the man's throat and shoved his face down just in case he tried to scream. He didn't.

Prosper wiped his blade off on the man's shirt and put it back into the sheath on his belt. Then he took the man's Henry and revolver and tossed them into the stream. He grabbed his own rifle.

"What'n hell's that noise, Buster? Somebody comin' across? The man paused for a moment, then yelled, "Buster! Answer me, dammit!"

Moments later, the speaker was plowing through the trees, and his nose ran into the curved butt of Prosper's Henry. He went down as if poleaxed, out and on the verge of dying with pieces of his septum and eye socket lancing into his brain.

"Damn," Prosper muttered. He hadn't planned to hit the man so hard. He wanted to question him as he had Buster, hoping for actual answers, but that was out of the question now. He pitched the man's weapons into the stream and moved on, heading away from the river before turning upstream again as quietly as he could. He stopped when he heard horses shuffling and the light jingling of bits. There were five horses, all saddled. He did not like the odds, even though he had evened them somewhat. Trouble was, he didn't know where the other three were.

A minute later, he got a fix on at least two of them and headed in the direction of where the shots had come from. He stopped when he saw movement, trying to decide whether to shoot the man in the back or give him a warning.

Then the man yelled, "Best give up, redskins. We're runnin' out of patience with you."

"Go to hell, white-eyes," Painted Bear shouted.

Prosper figured the Ute had moved as soon as the speaker fired two rounds from his rifle, and other shots came from two spots a little way back from the rocky stretch of bank that reached the stream.

That made Prosper's decision easier. Endangering the Ute warrior was one thing. Threatening Smoke Rising and Lives Again was an entirely different matter. He fired, putting a slug in the back of the man's head.

"Two to go," Prosper muttered as he headed upriver to where the other gunfire had come from.

A bullet thudded into the tree he was passing, two inches from his head, spraying him with bark. "Shit," he hissed as he whirled behind the tree, then scooted to his left to get behind another cottonwood. He dared not move again since he figured whoever had fired at him was watching for him to show himself even a little. A growing concern was the fifth man. With the stream running a few yards to his left, five horses making their usual noises, and a light wind blowing through the leaves, Prosper could not determine where that man was and whether he was circling around to get behind him.

Not content to squat here and wait to be caught

in a crossfire, he rapidly fired three shots from the Henry at where he thought the other gunman had fired from. Then he darted several feet to his right and knelt behind a thick weeping willow. He could see through the leaves after a fashion and hoped the other man or men could not see through them to where he was.

He spun at the sound of a twig breaking and moved a little farther around the tree trunk and watched where the noise had come from. He spotted a man weaving slowly from trunk to trunk, wary. Prosper raised his Henry, aimed, and...

Just before he fired, an arrow tore through the willow's branches not far from Prosper's head and landed in a tree several feet from the attacker. Prosper hesitated for only a moment before firing twice, hitting the man in the chest with both bullets.

Moments later, there was a crashing through the brush off to his left, heading in a diagonal away from him. Then came the sound of a horse galloping away. Prosper checked the horses; four remained. Then he went back and checked on the men who had been shot to be sure they were dead. They were. He threw the men's guns into the stream, then pulled the arrow from the tree trunk.

Satisfied that the danger was over, he shouted, "Painted Bear! Smoke! Come on across." As he waited for them, he tapped the arrow against his hand, wondering.

CHAPTER 8

"This is yours," Prosper said, handing Painted Bear the arrow.

"Yes."

"You either need to learn to shoot better or not to shoot through tree branches. That doesn't lend itself to much accuracy."

"I was tryin' to kill man tryin' to kill you."

"Almost got me by mistake, then."

"I try to kill him. Branches make arrow go bad."

"Like I said, either improve your aim or don't shoot through trees." He turned to the woman. "You think you can handle a few extra horses, Smoke?"

"If tied together, yes. Can't herd 'em."

"Wouldn't expect you to. They're over there beyond that thicket," he added, pointing. "These four boys don't need 'em anymore. I reckon John'll be pleased to have a few extra head."

"I take 'em. They mine," Painted Bear said.

"No, they ain't. You didn't do anything to earn 'em for one thing, and it'll help John pay for things he needs around the place with two—um, three—extra mouths to feed."

The Ute thought to argue but decided not to when he saw the hard look in Prosper's eyes.

"There's still a heap of daylight left," the bounty hunter said, "so we'll move on for a few hours. I hate to waste time, and I'd rather not set here with four bodies layin' about."

"I thought white-eyes always buried their dead," Painted Bear said.

"Usually. But these boys don't deserve it, and I ain't of a mood to take the time even if they did." He took his pistol back from Smoke Rising, then headed off to string the horses together. As he was doing so, he smiled when he saw Painted Bear prowling around the bodies, apparently looking to pick up one or more of the weapons from the corpses.

"These men do much shooting with no guns," Painted Bear said as Prosper finished his task.

"They had plenty of guns. Couldn't see any reason to keep 'em, so I tossed 'em all in the water when I was waiting for you to cross the stream. Didn't want the wrong folks finding 'em," Prosper added pointedly.

The Ute scowled, growled, and walked away, back stiff in anger.

Before long they were on their way again, Prosper nervously leading the way, followed by Smoke Rising with the baby in his cradleboard hanging from her saddle and five horses in tow, and then Painted Bear. Prosper did not like having the Ute warrior riding behind him, but he figured that if the other man who had attacked them was out there, he might not be so trigger-happy if he saw another white man instead of an Indian. Prosper was glad, though, that he had tossed the enemies' weapons away. And he was pretty sure Smoke Rising would keep her man from doing him any harm.

When they finally stopped that evening, it took Prosper, with little—very little—help from Painted Bear some time to unsaddle and tend all the horses, though the new mounts did not need as much care as those that had been ridden. The lack of help annoyed Prosper, as did the time it took to do the chores, and he considered leaving all the attackers' tack here and let the horses go bareback.

Smoke Rising must have sensed what he was thinking, and when he sat at the fire and gratefully accepted the mug of coffee she handed him, she said, "We make travois."

"What for?" he asked, surprised and a little confused.

"For saddles and things. Then not spend much time tendin' animals."

"Think we can get one of those horses to pull one?"

"Yes."

"No," Painted Bear interjected. "They're ridin' ponies, not haulin' ones."

Smoke Rising ignored him. "Not new horses. Old one used for supplies. Is meek, will pull travois good."

"You sure?"

"Yes."

"Even with saddlebags maybe full?"

"Empty some things, should be good."

Prosper nodded. "We'll start right after feedin'."

** ** ** ** **

Finished, Prosper said, "Let's go build us a travois, Painted Bear."

"Not done eatin'."

"Yes, you are."

"Warrior doesn't build travois. That women's work."

"Well, one Ute warrior is gonna build one, or at least help build one. Now get yourself up and moving."

"No."

"You know, boy, I'm plumb tired of your fractiousness. Now get your ass up and help me."

"Or what?"

"Or I'll kick your ass, which'll humiliate you in front of your woman."

"You can't do."

"You aim to try me, boy?"

Before the warrior could retort, Smoke Rising said, "You watch Lives Again. I help Elias."

Prosper smiled at the look of terror on Painted Bear's face.

"I not watch child either," the warrior said. "I have things to do."

"Like what?" Prosper asked. "Pluck the hairs out of your nose? Maybe paint your breechclout with drawins of all your mighty deeds? Oh, now I recall—you don't have any mighty deeds. All you got is a contrary disposition. What you don't have is any sense in your head or any sense of decency."

Prosper rose. "Well, reckon I can't expect anything out of you, boy, so sit here and feed your face whilst I do the work." He headed to where he kept a small ax and went to check out some likely trees. He hacked down two slender aspens, then cut off the branches. He got a rope and began lashing the ends of the logs together on an "X" shape.

Prosper smiled when Smoke Rising brought two of the outlaws' bedrolls over. With Lives Again in the cradleboard on the woman's back, the Ute helped fashion the bedrolls into a strong bed onto which to load the saddles and such.

As they worked, Smoke Rising asked, "How you know these people who take us in maybe? What they like?"

"Well, let's see. I was born east of here, like I said. Ma died a couple years later. Pa left me and my brothers and sisters in the Settlements and headed west with a fur trappin' brigade. He spent several years doing that before he returned to where our homestead had been, gathered up his children, married again, and moved us all to a new homestead."

The two secured the first bedroll and decided a second would be good.

"John went west to be a mountain man when he was young, but the trade was old, maybe in '36 or '37. That's where Pa met him and became his mentor, I guess you could say."

"What is 'mentor?'"

"A teacher in a way. Someone who helps another learn some kind of trade. Afterward, John went back east with Pa and helped 'round the farm and started learning other trades, like woodworkin', wheelwrightin', blacksmithin'. He was there for six years or so, then headed southwest on the Santa Fe Trail. He did that a couple times, then fought in the war against Mexico. After that, he stayed in Santa Fe, then Taos, and finally settled in an area along the Huerfano River. I was maybe fourteen or fifteen when he left."

Finished with the travois, Prosper and Smoke Rising began going through the dead men's saddlebags. Prosper got rid of all the weapons, though he kept the cartridges. They were hard to get, and Prosper was glad to have extra ones. Even though they were not easily available, he'd had his Starr revolver converted to a cartridge one because the Henry used the same shells. He also took powder and caps and lead, wrapped them in a piece of elk skin, and stuck them in his saddlebags. His backup pistol, the .36-caliber Pocket Colt he had lent to Smoke Rising that was back in his pocket now, was a cap-and-ball model.

"I visited John a few times, including once just before the war started," Prosper continued. "Ain't been back since, but I reckon if John and Matilda are still there, they'll be happy to take you three in."

They emptied another saddlebag of two old shirts and a pair of socks. Smoke Rising giggled at the latter, then asked, "What about woman Matilda?" She had a little trouble pronouncing the name.

Prosper smiled. "Matilda's a fine woman. You'll like her, I expect. Her Jicarilla name's Many Good

Things, though I can't for the life of me pronounce it in Jicarilla. She was born the same year I was. John spent some time with the Jicarilla, though I don't know how he met them. And since he could speak the language, he helped Kit Carson when he was the agent for the Jicarilla and your people. He sat out the recent war far's I know. Too many people needed him.

"Look, coffee!" Smoke Rising interrupted, holding up a bag of coffee beans.

"That'll help," Prosper agreed. Going through another bag, he found some silver dollars, gold eagles, and a few greenbacks. He pocketed it all.

"They met 'round 1854, maybe '55. She was twenty-four or maybe twenty-five and a widow. Her husband, a Jicarilla warrior, had been killed in a battle with the Mexicans. She had two children by him. When John married her, he took the young'uns in as his own. They been together ever since."

"Her life not different than mine."

"Some. She does all the women's work that other women, white, Mexican, and red, do, but she's more than that. She cares for other children, raises vegetables and such in a little garden, doctors the ailin', helps women with birthin'. And she does it all with a smile on her face, like you most times. She's the most jolly person I ever knew."

"I like."

"Like that she's jolly, or you smile like her?"

"Both." Her face clouded. "Not much smiles now."

"You afraid of me?" Prosper asked, concerned and shocked.

"No," the woman said hastily. "Not you. You make me smile."

"Painted Bear?"

She nodded and hung her head.

"He is a fractious son of a gun, that's certain. But things'll get better when you get to the Huerfano."

"I hope."

"I think he's so peevish because he needs to fart to let all that anger out." Prosper grinned.

"Fart?" Smoke Rising looked confused.

Prosper squinted as if in mild pain, made a pfffftttt sound, wiggled his rear end, and waved his hand behind him as if fanning away a bad smell.

Smoke Rising stood there for a moment as if still confused, then she giggled and finally let go a full-throated laugh.

Prosper grew serious. "He ain't hurtin' you or the child, is he?"

"No. He likes me. Not like Lives Again but not hurt him. He and..." She looked embarrassed again.

"I know, him and I are at loggerheads more often than not."

Once more, the woman looked confused. "What that mean?"

"Loggerheads?" When she nodded, he thought for a moment before saying, "Buttin' heads, like mountain sheep do during ruttin' season." He gently hit his fists together.

Smoke Rising nodded sadly.

"Must be hard on you, having two hardheaded men always tryin' to be the cock of the walk. The head stallion in the herd."

"Yes." She brightened and laughed again. "Maybe he go pfffftttt and will be nicer."

Prosper laughed too. "Maybe, Smoke, maybe."

They went back to their work and were soon finished.

CHAPTER 9

The ride went smoothly for the next several days. The horse pulling the travois gave them no trouble and docilely hauled its burden. The captured horses mostly behaved as well now that they had no saddles or riders on them.

A week out, however, they spent half a day going upriver to where they could safely cross and avoid a small but fast-flowing waterfall.

Prosper decided to make their night's camp there, though it was only midafternoon. They could all use a rest, he figured, and this was as pleasant a place as they were likely to find two hours or so away. They ate well on the elk Painted Bear had brought in and drank some coffee. They savored the latter since they were running short of it, even with the small supply they had found in the dead men's saddlebags.

The rest did them good, and they were a little sprightlier when they pushed on in the morning, following, as they had been, a nonexistent trail through the trees and brush and across mountain meadows, some small, some large. They were crossing one of the latter when half a dozen Ute warriors appeared out of the trees on the other side.

"Stop, Bear!" Prosper shouted when it looked as if the Ute was ready to bolt to join his fellow Utes.

The newcomers looked to have been ready to raise hair on the small traveling party until they recognized Painted Bear as one of their own. One of them rode forward slowly, stopping ten feet or so from Painted Bear.

Prosper moved up alongside Smoke Rising and directed her to pull forward with a nod of his head. The two were close enough to Painted Bear to have their horses nibble on the tail of the warrior's horse.

Painted Bear and the other Ute warrior started conversing in their own language.

"Do you know that other fella, Smoke?" Prosper asked.

"No. He's not of our band."

"What're the two of 'em sayin'?" Prosper asked.

"Other warrior asks what Painted Bear and I doing with you." She listened a moment. "Painted Bear says he captured the horses and you helpin' bring 'em to village."

"Why, that son of a..."

"Wait. Other one say he wants two horses to let us pass. Painted Bear say he'll give one."

"Like hell." Prosper pushed his horse forward until he was next to Painted Bear. The other Ute seems surprised. "You understand English?" Prosper asked.

The Ute solemnly nodded.

"What's your name?"

"Red Elk."

"Well, Red Elk, I know what this damn fool's been tellin' you, and I'm here to say you ain't gettin' any horses. Painted Bear here didn't capture 'em. I did. Killed four men to take 'em, white men who were attackin' us. This here fella doesn't have a thing to say about what happens with these horses."

Red Elk seemed shocked. "You refuse two, we," he waved a hand toward his companions, "take 'em."

"You try that, and there'll be at least a couple dead Utes decoratin' the grass here."

"This our land. You pay to pass."

"This is his land, too," Prosper said, pointing at Painted Bear. "And hers, and the child's."

"Baby belongs to you?" Red Elk asked, looking at Painted Bear.

The latter hesitated.

"Is mine," Smoke Rising said. "Father dead. Painted Bear help, take me as his woman to raise baby."

Red Elk sat, looking from one person to the other, apparently lost in thought. Finally he said, "You give one horse to pass."

"Maybe you didn't understand me, Red Elk. You ain't gettin' a horse to allow your own people to cross their land."

"Want only one pony. They pass without givin' horse. You give pony for you to pass."

"Nope. I'm helpin' these folks get somewhere, so I ain't payin' for passage, especially when someone demands it. I don't take kindly to demands."

Red Elk waved his hand, and his fellow warriors

began slowly moving forward.

"Now hold on a minute, Red Elk. There's no call for fightin' here, no call for anyone dying. Let me ask you this. Do you know John Higgins, the man the Utes and Jicarilla call Plenty Help? Fella who helped Colonel Carson run the agency for both people?"

"Yes." He gave Prosper a questioning look as his warriors spread out in a small semicircle behind him.

"That's where we're going. We're taking the child to Many Good Things for some spirit medicine."

It took only a few moments for Red Elk to nod. "You go. Give no pony."

"Obliged, Red Elk. I hope your medicine stays good."

The Ute nodded once, then turned his horse, and with his fellow warriors following, trotted away.

"You can join 'em if you want, Painted Bear," Prosper said, watching the Utes dwindle on the horizon.

The warrior looked longingly at the departing Utes, then looked at Smoke Rising, torn between the two. Finally he took off, galloping after his fellow Utes.

Smoke Rising sighed.

"You can go too if you want," Prosper added.

The woman looked wistfully at the fast-dwindling figure of Painted Bear. "I stay," she said quietly.

Prosper nodded. "Then let's get back on the move." As they moved across the meadow, he added, "You'll likely be better off without him, Smoke. You might love him, but I ain't so sure he really feels the same way about you."

"He good man mostly, but he warrior, so has own ways, ways of battle, ways of other warriors."

"He ought to be carin' for the women he loves. But that's not for me to say, I reckon."

Prosper thought Smoke Rising seemed fearful—or maybe lonely—that night as they made camp. He wasn't sure if she missed Painted Bear or if she was afraid Prosper might try to take advantage of her now that her Ute lover was gone.

She seemed better the next day, though still wary around him.

Prosper hated to let her ride alone with the baby and the horse in her care, but they needed meat. With Painted Bear gone, it was up to Prosper to supply it.

When he told her, she nodded, but as he prepared to leave, she asked worriedly, "You be back?"

"Soon's I can. I ain't about to leave you ridin' alone out here any longer than I have to."

She still looked worried. He smiled and put his hands on her shoulders. "I ain't about to leave, and I ain't about to take advantage of you. I think of you as my sister. I heard that some tribes don't let brother and sister be near each other, but white folks ain't that way. White men protect their sisters, and that's what I'll do for you. So don't you fret. Just keep those horses movin' slow. I'll get back soon's I can." He mounted and rode out nervously, taking one of the horses with him.

He was lucky and dropped an elk within half an hour. He rushed through butchering out enough meat to last them a couple of days. More than that, and it would go rancid in the warm weather. Then he hurried to catch up with Smoke Rising.

She looked frightened when he caught up to her, but her face showed relief when she realized it was him. He nodded at her. "We'll have some fine eatin' tonight."

With a smile, Smoke Rising urged her horse to go a little more briskly.

They did indeed eat well that night on fresh elk enhanced with herbs Smoke Rising had found along the way. "That was plumb good eatin', Smoke. I wish we had some coffee, though."

"Be happy," the woman chided him in a friendly manner.

"Yes, ma'am," he said with a smile.

** ** ** ** **

Prosper awoke with a start, though he moved little at first. He wasn't sure what had roused him, so he lay quietly trying to place it. Then Smoke Rising screamed, but it was cut off. Prosper rolled out of his blankets and came up with his pistol in hand. He glided toward where she slept on the other side of the fire from him. He saw someone bending over the woman, and a chill ran down his back.

A startled Lives Again squawked, pushing Prosper to hurry the last few steps. He thought he knew who it was. He reached out, grabbed the would-be attacker by the back of his buckskin shirt, yanked Painted Bear off Smoke Rising, and flung him to the ground.

The warrior started to rise, reaching for his knife or tomahawk, but Prosper cocking his revolver stopped the Ute.

"What the hell're you doing here, boy?"

"Come for Smoke Risin'."

"Should've come in the daytime and asked if she wanted to go with you 'stead of sneakin' 'round in the night scarin' the devil out of everyone."

"Didn't want you to know."

"Damn but you're an idiot. Lordy, I ought to just kill you here and now. It wasn't for Smoke Rising caring for you, I damn well would.

Painted Bear stayed silent.

"You ever think she might not want to go with you? After you run off like you did to be with those other warriors?"

Painted Bear did not respond.

"Why'd you come back, anyway?"

"Missed her," Painted Bear said angrily. "Think maybe you covered her while I was gone."

"Hell, no, you idiot. She's like a sister to me, and white men do not cover their sisters." He paused, then asked sharply, "Were you plannin' to take Lives Again along with Smoke?"

Prosper felt anger building inside. "You weren't, were you? You were gonna leave him here alone except for me, weren't you?"

"No, I would take Smoke Rising, she would bring Lives Again. Make family."

"I'm not sure I believe you, boy, but I can't prove different. Were you gonna take her off to join the other warriors?"

"No. Don't trust 'em."

"What'n hell were you gonna do? Just wander by

yourselves? You turned that notion down weeks ago when we first started travelin' together. You think the Utes east of your band will just take you in?"

"Yes."

"Hell, maybe they would. There's loco red people as much as there are white folks. You still should've asked Smoke if she wanted to go with you."

"I was tryin'."

"By wakin' her in the middle of the night to try and explain to her that you wanted to spirit her and Lives Again away to you don't know where? Without me knowin' it? That's a damn thick-headed notion. You should know that if you...well, I don't much give a damn about what you want. If Smoke wanted to go off with you or anyone else, I wouldn't stop her. I likely would try to talk her out of it if I thought it was an imprudent idea. And the way you acted the past couple weeks, I think leavin' with you would be really ill-advised."

Painted Bear just lay there, quiet.

"Look, Bear, I figure we got two more days on the trail 'til we get to my friend's place. Just go along peaceable and not give me any trouble. When we get there, you can decide what you want to do. Smoke can also decide what she wants to do. I hope that if you leave, Smoke stays behind. She and Lives Again'll be much better off with John and Matilda than they would with you. Now get up, and give me your bow and quiver."

"I not give up my weapons," Painted Bear snapped.

"You give me any more sass, and not only will I take your bow and quiver full of arrows, I'll take away your knife and tomahawk, too."

"Do it, Painted Bear," Smoke Rising pleaded. "Is better for all."

The Ute looked at her. He was humiliated and wanted to attack Prosper, but he knew that would get him killed. He sighed, but with barely bottled rage, he handed over his bow and quiver of arrows.

"Now get some sleep. We'll pull out early. Quicker we get moving, the quicker we'll get where we're going. The less time you and me are together, the better."

CHAPTER 10

The small caravan moved through the great open wooden doors in the tall adobe wall surrounding what amounted to a village. The house was straight across from the entrance, a two-story adobe with a colorful door and window casings. Bright red ristras hung from the exposed vigas protruding from the roof under the thatched portico. A small shaded courtyard was to the right, and to the right of that was a truck garden with a variety of vegetables and herbs growing. On the left against the front wall of the compound was an adobe barn with a corral behind it stretching almost to the back wall. Next to the barn sat several wagons in various states of repair. At the far end of the corral were a pigpen and chicken coop. Beyond the back wall, horses and cattle grazed under the watchful eye of two or three men, or perhaps boys, Prosper thought. Beyond the left wall was a farm where wheat, corn, beans, pumpkins, and more were being tended by both men and women. Against the right-side wall was a long, low open-faced series of workshops, and against the wall to the right of the gate was a bunkhouse for single laborers and guests. Outside the walls on the eastern side were perhaps a dozen small houses where married laborers and their families lived. A cantina and a store were about a quarter-mile outside the eastern wall.

As they moved nearer to the house, the hammering and clanging coming from the open workshops stopped as workmen stood and watched. A tall, slender man came out of the end workshop, wiping his brow with a bandanna taken from around his neck. He stopped, and a grin began to form. "Elias? That you?"

"Sure enough, John."

"Well, it's been an age since you last come by. Come on, we'll go in the house, have some food and cold drinks, get that baby some shade," he said as he pointed at Lives Again, who had just announced his presence with a small squawk.

As he walked beside Prosper, Higgins called, "Roberto, José, get on over here and take care of these animals." Though it was shouted, there was no condescension in the voice.

Two young men hurried out of the workshops. Prosper figured they were apprentices since they were too young to be a blacksmith and a carpenter. When they reached the house and started to dismount, Higgins yelled again, "Matilda! Come see who's come to visit."

A short, plump woman came out of the house, wiping her hands on an apron. "What're you yellin' about, old man?" She spotted Prosper. "Elias!"

"One and the same, Matilda."

"And as you can see, he's brought company."

"Come, come," Matilda said. Though she had lived with Higgins among English- and Spanish-speaking people and she could speak both, her words were still tinged with the cadence of her native Jicarilla, though her words and phrases bore more resemblance to English than any other language. She stepped forward and tossed an ample arm over Smoke Rising's shoulders. "Come, child, let's get you and that young'un out of this infernal sun." She led the Ute away.

"Still the mother hen, eh, John?"

"That she is." He grinned. "Wouldn't have it any other way, though."

"Where are your young'uns?"

"Felix is over there learnin' to make saddles; Merry and Samuel are in Santa Fe to get some education. Merry'll be back soon. She's about marryin' age now, and we don't want to leave her on her own down there with all the temptations. Lilith is among these little heathens," he added with a wave at the children playing in the yard, "runnin' around here with some of the other kids. Little Charlotte," he said with a hitch in his voice, "has gone to meet her Maker."

"No! Damn, John, I am truly sorry."

"It's been almost a year and a half, and we've moved on mostly. Have to." The words were brave, but his tone was sad. "Don't say anything in front of Matilda, though."

"I sure won't."

"And who's this strappin' young man?"

"His name's Painted Bear. He ain't speakin' to me much of late," Prosper said with a shrug.

"Welcome to my lodge, Painted Bear. We're glad to have you visit," he said in Ute, surprising the warrior.

Painted Bear muttered something in his own language.

"What'd he say?" Prosper asked.

"Said you're a disreputable man, as am I, and so are all white men." He grinned. "No wonder he ain't talkin' to you." He looked at Painted Bear and said in Ute, "Elias is a white man, but I'm only half-white. But you're welcome despite your feelin's about us, so come on in."

Inside was a long table with three chairs on each side and one at each end. Smoke Rising sat in one while Matilda fussed over the baby.

"Leave that child be, woman, and bring us some food," Higgins said in a friendly tone.

"Oh, hush, old man," Matilda responded, though she did set about putting bowls on the table.

The three men sat. "You want coffee, Elias? Just water after hot travelin', maybe some corn..."

"Coffee'll do," Prosper said, giving a slight nod at Painted Bear.

Higgins nodded. He wouldn't have given the Ute any alcohol, but there was no need to introduce it into the conversation.

Smoke Rising stood, aiming to help Matilda, even with the baby on her hip. He had been taken out of his cradleboard within moments of being in the house.

"No, no," the older woman said. "You just sit and let old Matilda take care of things." Smoke Rising sat, looking at Prosper as if she were uncomfortable. He smiled at her, and she relaxed a little.

Matilda soon had bowls with steaming bean and beef chili and fry bread on the table in front of the visitors. Coffee appeared in mugs alongside the bowls.

Prosper dug right in, though Painted Bear looked at the food with disdain, and Smoke Rising appeared uncertain. "It's good," Prosper said to her.

Smoke Rising tentatively tried it, then smiled and ate a few spoonsful with more enthusiasm. Then the fiery spices hit her, and she looked around wildly. Prosper and the Higginses laughed, and Matilda handed her a glass of milk, something else Smoke Rising had never had before. She gulped down a few mouthfuls, not caring what it was. Relieved, she looked at the chili warily and ate with a little more discretion, interspersing spoonsful with mouthfuls of milk.

"Reckon introductions should be made," Prosper said around mouthfuls of chili. He pointed with his spoon at the warrior. "He's Painted Bear." The spoon moved to point at the young woman. "And she's Smoke Rising. The infant is Lives Again."

"I'm John Higgins," the owner said, "and Matilda there's my wife." He shook his head in faux disappointment. "All these years we been married, and she's still a thorn in my side."

"You want your bed warmed tonight, you can get one of the cows in here."

Husband and wife laughed. They were joined by Prosper. Smoke Rising looked confused, and Painted Bear still had an angry cast to his face.

Finally the food was done with, and they all—except Painted Bear—relaxed a bit. Higgins pulled out a pipe, filled it, and lit it, then asked, "So what brings you to 'Higginsville?'"

"That's what you call this old place?" Prosper sputtered.

"Sounds better than John and Matilda's place on the Huerfano River," Higgins said with a laugh.

"Reckon it does." Prosper chuckled. "Well, I'm hopin' you'll take in Painted Bear and Smoke Rising. Oh, and Lives Again, too, of course."

"Be glad to take in Smoke Rising and the baby. I ain't so sure about Painted Bear. The young fella looks like he wants to be somewhere else."

"Reckon he does. But he says he loves Smoke Rising and wants to be with her. Says he'll work doing whatever he can."

"Lord, I ain't heard such a heapin' pile of mule biscuits in a long time."

Prosper smiled ruefully. "When he first joined us and I figured we could come here, he did say all that. In the few weeks on the trail, however, he's gone back to thinkin' he should be out there raidin' with the other Utes. He's also pissed that I humiliated him a couple times."

"Any man would be."

Prosper nodded. "Some of us learn through that if it's done away from other folk, which this was. Others don't learn."

"Well, what do you say, Painted Bear?" Higgins asked. "You willin' to stay here and learn a trade."

The Ute glanced at Smoke Rising, who looked back with pleading in her eyes.

"I do. No farmin', though."

"No farmin'. First few days, we'll let you try your hand at various things, see if you like any or come naturally to one. After that, we'll figure out something for you."

Painted Bear just grunted approval.

"How'd you come up with these two, ah, three, Elias?"

"Found Lives Again—Smoke named him—floatin' in a basket on a lake. I fished him out and went lookin' for his people. I found a band, but the chief said the baby was cursed, and his people didn't want anything to do with him. Said he was responsible for a bunch of deaths when Arapahos attacked a small village and some folks drowned trying to get away. Said he was bad medicine."

"Cursed? Damn fools if they believe that. I never heard the Utes thinkin' such a thing." A sly grin crossed his face. "Boys ain't cursed, just women. Particularly Jicarilla women."

Matilda threw a napkin at him, and they all enjoyed another laugh.

"I made the chief send me out a young woman to be a wet nurse to the little fella."

"Smoke Rising?" Matilda asked.

"Yup. Made him give us some supplies, too."

"How'd Painted Bear come into this?" Higgins asked.

"Attacked me a few days after I left the chief. Said he loved Smoke and wanted to marry her, but she already had a husband who didn't love her and blamed her for the death of their infant." He cast a sidelong glance at Matilda, whose face had darkened in sadness. "Bear thought I'd be takin' Smoke to my bed..."

"Did you?" Matilda asked harshly, the sadness from the talk of a child's death fading.

"No. I ain't that kind of man."

"All men are that kind of man," Matilda said, but she grinned.

"So he decided to join our merry little group. They had nowhere else to go, really. If one band thought the baby was bad medicine, it could be that others would feel the same. Plus, there was the little problem of Smoke's nasty husband. Took a couple days, then I thought of you and Matilda. Figured you could train him to do something useful, something he could use after the rest of his people are penned up. Smoke seemed pleased with the idea, especially when I told her about Matilda."

"Probably all lies," Matilda said, but she grinned in pride and patted the Ute woman's hand.

"Bear agreed at the time, but I ain't so sure he still feels the same way. I ain't worried about Smoke. She's a good young woman and will be a big help around here. But if Bear don't take to whatever trade you try to teach him, I'm gonna be powerful upset that I dropped him on you, John."

"Don't worry about that, Elias. He doesn't work out, it'll be on him, not on you."

"And I don't figure Lives Again'll give you any trouble," Prosper said with a laugh. "At least, not for a few years anyway."

Everyone chuckled except Painted Bear.

"You get those extra horses from the Ute chief?"

"Nope. He gave us one at my urging to carry supplies. The others come from a bunch of skunks who attacked us on the trail."

"I take it you disposed of 'em?"

"Yup. Four of the five, anyway. The fifth took off runnin'. Might still be doin' so. Took the horses and all the tack, plus the few useful or worthwhile things they had in their saddlebags. You can have it all. Sell it for whatever you can get for it. Count it as payment for taking in these three."

"Hell, Elias, you should know we don't expect to be paid for takin' people in. They'll earn their keep."

"Reckon they will, but I have no use for it all, though I suppose I could herd the horses and have one pull a travois down to Taos and sell 'em. But I got no hankerin' to do such."

"Pueblo's a far sight closer than Taos. We can sell 'em either place and wire you the money somewhere. Horses and tack will sell readily 'round here."

Prosper thought that over, then shook his head. "Last bounty I picked up in Salt Lake City was handsome, so I'm set with cash for a spell." He paused again, thinking, then said, "Tell you what, John. Take half the money for you and Matilda. Do what you want with it. Maybe put an addition on the house, buy more land. Take the other half and put it aside for Lilith's and Lives Again's education."

"By golly, that's a fine idea," Higgins said, with Matilda throwing in her wholehearted support.

"You got some room out there in the single workers' quarters where we could all bed down tonight?"

"This young woman and this infant are not going anywhere but to a bedroom upstairs," Matilda said firmly.

Higgins chuckled. "We got plenty of room for you and Painted Bear in here. He can stay with Smoke if she's of a mind to allow it. He can move out to the quarters tomorrow. If he proves to be a good worker, we'll set him, Smoke, and Lives Again up in one of the houses outside the walls. You and Smoke and the baby can stay here in the house as long as you want."

"Obliged, John, Matilda."

"Well, it's much too early for headin' for bed," Higgins said. "I got to get back to work. Even though it's been a spell, you should know your way around. Maybe you can show Bear the place."

Prosper nodded.

CHAPTER 11

"How's Painted Bear doing, John?" Elias Prosper asked as he sat at the table around dusk. He had just come back from an almost three-week trip down to Taos to pick up a wagonload of supplies.

"Shows some talent for woodworkin'," John Higgins said. "But I'm leery of having him handle some of the tools."

"Understandable." He nodded thanks to Matilda, who had just served him a plate brimming with pork chops and potatoes.

"He's one of the best I ever had at carin' for the horses, but I don't trust him with the animals either. Once a horse thief, always a horse thief."

"Can't argue with that, John. Not surprised, though, that he handles the animals well."

"I ain't either, but what to do with him is something of a conundrum."

"You'll figure it out. It's only been a few weeks," Prosper said around mouthfuls of food.

"I know, but I've got good men, good families

here, and I don't need him stirrin' up trouble."

"Nobody does. How's Smoke Rising and Lives Again?"

"The girl is such a delight," Matilda said with a wide smile. "Helpful 'round here, willin' to do just about anything to make my work easier. And that boy is fat and sassy. Just the opposite of my husband, who's skinny and grumpy."

Prosper grinned. "They still living here in the house?"

"Nope," Higgins said, looking both relieved and worried. "Set her and Painted Bear up in one of the houses outside a few days after you headed down to Taos. Not real sure how they're doin', not bein' used to livin' in a house instead of a tipi. But I ain't heard no complaints."

"Smoke Rising—we call her Laura—wouldn't complain if the roof fell in on her. Painted Bear—Honus now, after John's grandad—I ain't so sure of. He ain't happy, but he's been keepin' it to himself. Laura ain't had a scratch on her, so I reckon he ain't abusin' her any."

"Damn good thing, too," Higgins added.

Prosper nodded. "You see her bruised or anything while I'm here, you fetch me directly."

"I'll handle it," Higgins said.

"Not while I'm here, you won't."

"How long you plannin' on stayin'?" Matilda asked. "You're more than welcome to stay as long as you like. You know that, but I know you to be a footloose man with the itch to travel."

"I am that. Need to make some money, too,

before much longer."

Higgins grinned. "I could put you to work here."

"I'd made a right good saddler, eh?" Prosper said with a laugh.

"Ah, well," Matilda said in mock resignation, "here I was hopin' you'd help me with my kitchen chores."

"I reckon I'll stay on another few weeks maybe. Give me time to rest up after travelin' from California and dealin' with Painted Bear on the trip here."

"Well," Higgins said, standing, "you might be a free man, Elias, but I've got tasks to handle before full dark comes. A man's work is never done," he added with a wink.

"Hah! A man don't do half the work a woman does, John Higgins, and you well know it."

"Reckon I do, woman, reckon I do." He clapped his hat on, kissed Matilda on the cheek, and headed out, passing two young Mexican girls coming in with pails of fresh milk.

Matilda gathered up the plate and cup Prosper had used and headed to the kitchen with them. Prosper took the hint and went outside. He sat on the porch, watching over the tranquil scene: horses being brought in from the pasture into the corral or barn, the men putting their tools away after the day's work and drifting toward their homes outside the walled town, children running about the plaza, and lights going on in the small free-standing cantina a quarter-mile west of the hacienda. There were many smells, some agreeable, like the aroma of spicy food cooking, some unpleasant but natural like horse and cow manure.

It might be pleasurable to have a life here like this, Prosper thought. For about two minutes. He laughed inwardly. He would be bored to death with such a life within a week or two.

** ** ** ** **

Ten days later, as Prosper sat down to breakfast with Higgins and Matilda, he said, "Reckon I'll be pullin' out today."

Higgins nodded sadly. "We'll miss you 'round here, even if you are a lazy, work-avoidin' fella. It's a good thing your saintly father ain't still alive…is he? He'd be powerful ashamed of you." He laughed.

"If he was—he ain't—he'd throw me out of his house and make you take me in," Prosper said, also laughing.

"Oh, you two," Matilda said with a sigh, but she smiled. Growing more serious, she asked, "You are aimin' to say goodbye to Laura and Juan—Lives Again—ain't you?"

"Nah, I thought I'd just sneak out so she won't yell at me like you're aimin' to do," Prosper said with a chuckle. "Of course I aim to bid her farewell. I told her along the trail that I thought of her as my sister, so I couldn't go off without sayin' something."

"Good."

Prosper wanted to bid farewell to Smoke Rising, but he also dreaded it. He loved her, and while he knew John and Matilda Higgins would care for her and watch over her, Prosper still worried about Painted Bear. He smiled when he considered what the Ute thought of the name "Honus." Prosper was sure he was not pleased.

Finally, though, he could put it off no longer. His horse was saddled and his packhorse loaded with enough supplies for a week, he mounted and waved at Matilda, who was on the porch, then rode over to where Higgins was working in his wheelwright shop.

"Know where you're headed, Elias?" Higgins asked.

"Nope."

"Head north, and you'll reach then Arkansas in less than a day. If you head upriver, you'll get to Pueblo soon. Maybe even tonight, dependin' on how fast you're travelin'. Head downriver, and you'll have a hell of a lot of empty before you get to some towns in Kansas. Worse, though, the Cheyenne and Arapaho are still on the prowl all across the prairie. They went on the warpath after a bunch of women and kids were massacred by a territorial militia over at Sand Creek a year and a half ago. Not as bad as last year, but still on the prod."

"Good to know. Don't know as if I would've gone that way anyway, but now I'll think some on it before I decided to risk it."

"If you do head north, best bet is to go to Pueblo. You can follow the Front Range north to Denver if you're of a mind to see a bigger city. Of course, you could always head south to Taos or Santa Fe."

"Well, I'll get where I'm going when I get there," Prosper said with a grin.

"And you won't be late gettin' there, neither. Adios, Elias. Or rather, vaya con Dios."

"If he'll have me, I reckon I don't mind if he rides along. See ya, John." The two shook hands, and Prosper headed through the big gates and turned left. In minutes he reached the house shared by Smoke Rising and Painted Bear. He still could not get a handle on calling them "Laura" and "Honus." He dismounted and knocked on the door.

Smoke Rising opened the door cautiously until she saw who it was. She smiled widely. "Come in, Elias. I happy you came."

He did so, then said, "I can't stay, Smoke. I'm headin' out and wanted to say goodbye to you and Lives Again."

"He Juan now," the Ute said, melancholy creeping over her face.

"I know. But to me, he'll always be Lives Again, and you'll always be Smoke Rising." He smiled.

She returned it, but there was little joy in it, just a deepening sadness.

"But I reckon I can call Painted Bear 'Honus.'" He grinned.

Smoke Rising could not hold back a giggle. She turned and picked up Lives Again from his cradle. The baby protested until the woman softly spoke a few words to him.

Prosper smiled and ran a finger down the baby's chubby cheek, bringing him back to the day he had found the baby. "You be a good boy for your mama, little fella." To the bounty hunter, his voice sounded a little lost. "Well, I'll be going. You take good care of Lives Again, and yourself too. If Painted Bear gives you any trouble at all, you go to John and Matilda.

They'll take care of you and make Honus stop whatever he's doing to hurt you."

"You'll come back to see us?"

"Yup. Got to keep an eye on that little fella as he grows."

Still sad, Smoke Rising stretched onto her toes to plant a sisterly kiss on Prosper's fresh-shaven face, then hugged him with one arm, the other still holding the baby. "Que el Gran Espíritu te acompañe, hermano mayor. May the Great Spirit ride with you, big brother." She broke away and began to close the door.

Prosper suspected she was crying. He couldn't blame her; he felt like doing the same. He would miss Smoke Rising and even Lives Again. He wouldn't miss Painted Bear. He mounted and rode on, heading north in not much of a hurry.

Almost two weeks later, he rode into Denver and was impressed by its big-city atmosphere, at least compared to Pueblo. He stabled his horses, found a hotel, and then had himself a spree—a shave, a haircut, a new set of clothes, a few good meals, some time in different saloons, and more time in a few bordellos.

By then, though, he was running low on money but had an abundance of boredom. He stopped by the city marshal's office and asked to see the wanted posters. The deputy on duty handed him a sheaf. "Have at it, friend."

"Any notable ones?"

"Big rewards, you mean?"

"Why else would I be chasin' outlaws?"

The deputy picked out a few and handed them to Prosper one by one. "Clark Bascom, train robbery, two hundred fifty. Gordon Munro, three murders, two train robberies, three stage robberies, eight hundred dollars. Mike Specter, murder, assault, several bank robberies, six hundred. Mort Anglin, raped two women, killed at least one man, also six hundred. Hugh Maples, two bank robberies, four hundred. Need more?"

"That'll do for now. Any idea where I can find 'em?"

"You're a bounty hunter. Find 'em yourself."

"Friendly cuss, ain't you? Where'd they pull their latest deviltry?"

"Sure I'm friendly. Don't like bounty hunters, though."

"Wasn't for bounty hunters, you'd have to get off your lazy ass and run down these miscreants yourself. Now, where'd these fellas last cause trouble 'round here?"

"'Round here, only Maples, who robbed banks in Central City and Idaho Springs to the west, and Specter. He killed a couple workers at a stage station fifty miles northeast. Rest of 'em haven't caused trouble in these parts for a while."

"Thanks." Prosper went back to his room and looked over the flyers. They were a desperate bunch of men, and the rewards on them were well-deserved.

CHAPTER 12

It was just after noon when Elias Prosper rode into the small camp. Several hardscrabble miners were sitting around a fire, eating. "Howdy," he said.

The men looked askance at him as a possible competitor for their panning, then realized that dressed and equipped as he was, he was not. They still thought he could be a claim jumper, though they had no claims worthy of jumping.

"Howdy," one of the men responded. "Passin' through?"

"Yup. Lookin' for a fella. Mind if I maybe share a bite?"

"We ain't got much, just some beans and stale biscuits, but you're welcome to have a little."

"Obliged," Prosper said, dismounting. He scooped some beans onto a plate one of the men handed him while another plopped a biscuit on top. Another filled a tin mug with coffee and set it down next to him.

Prosper wasn't all that hungry, but he figured

being friendly might bring him some information on the man he was chasing. He finished the food, burped, and set the plate down. "Ain't the best meal I ever had, but it ain't near the worst, either." He rose and walked to his packhorse, aware of the grumbling behind him as the miners figured he was a rotten enough man to not even thank them for the meal, as poor as it had been. But he pulled something out of a pack, turned around, and went back to the fire. He tossed a buckskin sack at the man who appeared to be the leader.

"Coffee," he said. "Don't know how much you have left, but that should tide you over for a week or so, maybe more if you go easy on it."

The men's faces lit up. "Well, thankee, Mr....?"

"Elias Prosper."

"I'm Horace Crump. My friends there are Ole Ingebrigtsen, Hog Wolk, and Chuck McKenzie."

"Hog?"

"Raised hogs back east before I come out here to seek my fortune."

Prosper nodded. "From the looks of it, maybe you should have stayed back east raising hogs."

"I reckon there's a heap of truth in that, Mr. Prosper. Ain't had much luck here so far."

"Why don't you boys pull up stakes and either head back to wherever your homes are or maybe try another place to seek your fortune?"

"Goin' home'd be too humiliatin'," Crump said. "Most folks we know back there told us we were damn fools to come out here. Hate to go back and prove 'em right."

"What about tryin' some other place to pan?"

"We've tried a few other places," Wolk said. "We're near ready to give up on this place. We found a little color here and thought maybe we'd struck it rich, but the color faded right quick."

Suddenly Crump held up a hand and hissed, "Quiet." When Ingebrigtsen gave him a questioning look, he whispered, "Somebody's out there."

"A claim jumper?" McKenzie asked in the same low tone.

"Might be." Crump rose and headed toward the brush, pulling an old revolver from a ratty holster hanging awkwardly from his hip. Minutes later he came back, gently pushing another man in front of him.

The newcomer's glance flickered from one man to the other, hesitating on Prosper a mite longer than the others, fear in his eyes.

"Don't look like a claim jumper to me," McKenzie said.

"Reckon not," Crump agreed. To the new man, he said, "Sit. There ain't much left, but you can have what little's there."

As the man sat and dug into the last of the beans, Crump asked, "What's your name, mister?"

"Hugh..." He hesitated, shooting a sideways look at Prosper. "Maples."

"What're you doin' out here, Mr. Maples? You don't look like no tin pan, and there's nothin' else out here but us poor prospectors."

"I'm... I'm..."

"He's hiding out from the law is what he's

doing," Prosper said.

"You the law?" McKenzie asked.

"Not directly."

"Bounty man?"

"Yup. And this is the fella I was searching for." Prosper looked at Maples. "Looks like your fortunes have taken a powerful downturn since you pulled those bank robberies in Central City and Idaho Springs. What'd you get in those jobs? Fifty thousand? Sixty?"

"Fifty-six thousand," Maples said with a dose of pride that vanished quickly.

"You robbed two banks of more'n fifty thousand bucks, and you're out here in the brush cadgin' meals off some dirt-poor tin-panners?" Ingebrigtsen asked, his surprise mixed with anger.

Maples nodded glumly.

"What'n hell happened to all that money?" Wolk asked.

Maples gave him a wry grin. "Pissed much of it away on cards, whiskey, and whores. Had a sprightly good time for a spell. I was heading for Golden when I was waylaid by my former partners, who knocked me on the head and took what was left of the money. Left me out there to die. I been stumblin' 'round out here for a day or two. Can't rightly remember."

"Seems like a comeuppance that was well-deserved," McKenzie said indignantly.

"Reckon so."

"Well," Prosper said almost cheerfully, "since you were heading for Golden, I'll just escort you there. Be a long walk for you, but I can't say as that bothers me."

"What's the bounty on him?" Wolk asked.

"Only four hundred."

"Only four hundred? Hell, that's a heap of money as far as we're concerned."

"It sure is," Crump said, eyes showing his sudden greed.

Prosper stared at him. "You boys don't really want to challenge me, do you?" His hand edged toward his holstered Starr.44.

"Reckon not," Crump grumbled.

"All right, Mr. Maples, it's time we were on the trail. Plenty of daylight left, and you've just been fed."

"I ain't quite finished yet."

"Yes, you are." Prosper grabbed Maples by the shirt collar, hauled him up, and gave him a shove toward his horse. He tied Maples' hands behind his back and put a slip-knot loop around his neck. Then he searched the man for weapons, finding a two-shot derringer in a vest pocket. "Lost your six-shooter too?"

"Yeah," Maples muttered.

"You are one sorry outlaw, Mr. Maples. A real embarrassment to other outlaws." Prosper laughed. He pulled some coins from a pocket and tossed a gold double eagle to each man. "Ain't much of a grubstake, but it'll get you some supplies if you get to a town. Enough to keep your search up for a few more weeks, anyway. Farewell." He mounted and moved out slowly, tugging on the rope around Maples' neck.

** ** ** ** **

Nine days later, Prosper towed his prisoner into the Colorado Territorial capital of Golden. He was glad Maples had given him no trouble on the journey, and he was glad he had been able to bring the outlaw in alive instead of dead. Prosper did not cotton to killing, though he was quite efficient at it when called upon.

He found a U.S. deputy marshal and handed Maples over to him. After the lawman put the man in a cell, he asked, "I don't suppose you found any of the money from the robberies on him, did you?"

To Prosper, the deputy sounded suspicious. "Does it look like he had thousands of dollars on him?" he countered.

"Reckon not. Still..."

"I found him wanderin' up in the mountains, lookin' like he does now. He had no money and no gun other than that derringer I gave you. He wandered into some tin pans' camp while I was there. Maples was starvin', and the prospectors let him have the last of their beans from the noon meal. I had just finished eatin' with those boys and was talkin' to 'em when Maples showed up. I let him eat, then proceeded to escort him here."

"Sounds mighty damn fortunate for you."

"Sometimes it happens that way. Not often, but occasionally."

"Such circumstances sound mighty suspicious."

"Look, pard, I don't give a good goddamn if you are a federal marshal. I don't take kindly to anyone calling me a thief."

"I didn't call you..."

"You sure as hell did, even if you didn't use those words, and I don't like it even one little bit. You make another accusation like that, and I'll shoot you dead here and now."

"That'll get you hanged," the lawman said with a smirk.

"I'll take my chances that the law dog who comes after me will have more sense and know what kind of fool you are."

"You're makin' me angry, mister."

"That's your account, not mine. I'm already angry, so maybe it's good that you're catchin' up. Maybe you ain't capable, but if you are, use your head, dammit. If he had thousands of dollars on him and I caught him out there up in the mountains wanderin' around and I took the money, do you really figure I'd drag him along for a week and a half for a four-hundred-dollar reward?"

"Reckon not," the lawman admitted, though he was not happy about it.

"No reckonin' about it, Marshal. I would've shot him dead out there, taken the money, and gone off and had me a spree in Denver or someplace. Or, if he had most of the money on him, I might've retired and gone into another line of work."

"He tell you where the money was? Maybe he buried it somewhere and was plannin' to go back and get it, but you caught him. Maybe you know where it's buried, and you'll be headin' there as soon as you leave here."

"Goddamn, Marshal, I've seen tree stumps that had more sense than you. Same thing. If he had told me he buried it and where it was, I would've made him take me there. Once I got the money, I would've shot him and gone off to live a good life on the cash."

"He tell you what happened to the money?"

"Said he spent some of it on a spree and was headin' somewhere else when his former partners caught up with him, took the money, his horse, and his gun, and left him to wander out there."

"And you believe him?"

"Yup. I checked him to make sure he wasn't armed. If he had the money on him, especially that much of it, I would've found it. If he buried it somewhere, there's no reason to tell me where it was."

"Bribe you to let him go."

"Possible, I reckon. But I figure if he had buried it somewhere, he'd not tell anyone. Robbery's gonna get him a stretch in the territorial prison, not hanged. He'd be out in a few years and go get his ill-gotten gains."

"Then..."

"And if he did bury it, why would he have gotten rid of his horse, thrown away his gun, and gone wanderin' around the hills? Even a damn fool like you should be able to see that."

"Just get your ass out of my office."

"I don't reckon it's really your office, you being just a deputy. But I will mosey on, considerin' the company here ain't worthy of my time." He grinned insolently. "I'll be back tomorrow for the reward money."

"What makes you think you'll get the reward money now that Maples is locked up in my jail here?"

Again he sneered.

"Reckon I'll have to talk to the actual marshal. Could be he's not as much of a horse's ass as you are." Prosper smiled despite his anger.

"You think he's gonna take the word of a no-'count saddle tramp over one of his deputies?"

"Yes, if that deputy is you. 'Course, he may be as big a simpleton as you, considerin' he was fool enough to hire a goat turd like you."

"Get out. I'm tired of dealin' with you."

"Same could be said for me." His voice grew harsh. "Like I said, I'll be back tomorrow. Have the money ready for me." With a last disrespectful smile, Prosper turned and left.

CHAPTER 13

"You know the deputy U.S. marshal here?" Prosper asked the bartender.

"Might," the man responded noncommittally, but he jerked his head as if signaling someone. "Why're you asking?"

"Because..."

"Something I can help you with, mister?" a burly, well-dressed man asked, stopping beside Prosper.

"Who're you?" Prosper asked.

"Could ask the same of you."

"I asked first."

The man smiled. "Chester Bradbury, U.S. marshal for Colorado Territory." He pulled open his frock coat to show the badge.

"The actual marshal, eh, not a deputy?"

"Chosen by President Johnson himself, Lord bless him."

To Prosper, the marshal didn't seem all that serious about the last. "Political appointee, eh?"

Bradbury did not seem bothered by the reference.

"Name's Elias Prosper." He held out his hand, and Bradbury shook it.

"So, why are you interested in my deputy, Mr. Prosper?"

"I was wonderin' why such a damn fool was hired. Doesn't seem like a hard-workin', conscientious lawman to me."

"Can't argue with that," Bradbury said with a chuckle. "What dealings have you had with him?"

"Brought in a prisoner a bit ago and said I'd expect the bounty by tomorrow. He didn't like that. I figure he's considerin' keepin' it for himself, tellin' folks he captured Maples."

"Hugh Maples?"

"One and the same."

"Where'd you find him?"

"Week and a half northwest of here. He stumbled into a small camp of tin pans. Was in poor shape, on foot, clothes worn through, hungry. I was fortunate enough to be there at the time and escorted him back here."

"Find any of the money?"

Prosper's darkened as his anger returned. "Your minion asked the same. Hinted that I took the money."

"Did you?" Bradbury's expression was bland, though there was a hint of steel in the words.

"What do you think? Same as I told your deputy. If he had had the money on him, do you think I would've dragged that bedraggled polecat all the way back here for a four-hundred-dollar reward?"

Bradbury grinned. "That would be mighty damn

foolish, I'd say, and you don't seem like a fool to me."

Prosper raised his mug of beer in a gesture of thanks, though it was a bit sarcastic. "Join me?" he asked.

"Don't mind if I do." Bradbury beckoned to the bartender, and moments later, a beer appeared before him.

"So, why'd you hire such a horse's ass?"

"Deputies are hard to find. Not too many folks around here want the responsibility of chasing outlaws."

"I would guess that...what the hell's his name, anyway? He never did say."

"Ambrose Armentrout."

Prosper spat beer. "Ambrose Armentrout?"

"Yup." Bradbury chuckled.

"As I was sayin', Marshal Armentrout doesn't seem like the type of lawman to go out chasin' outlaws unless it's someone who's wanted for kickin' his dog."

Bradbury laughed. "Even then, he'd hesitate and want a posse with him."

"Can't you find some other deputy?"

"I have two others, one working out of Hot Sulphur Springs and the other out of Cache Creek. Each of 'em covers a heap of territory. Armentrout is supposed to handle things east of Denver, but these days, it's dangerous out there on the plains. It amazes me that farmers and small ranchers remain out there with all the troubles of the past couple years."

"I suppose livin' out there's not much worse than huntin' dangerous men for a livin'."

"Ain't likely that some outlaw will try to lift your hair."

"Reckon that's true."

"How about I hire you, Mr. Prosper? You seem smart, and I figure you're a tough customer to do what you do and be successful at it, which apparently you are."

"I think I'll have to turn you down on that offer, Marshal."

"Why?" Bradbury didn't seem surprised.

"It's just as much risk as what I do now, and the pay's a hell of a lot less."

"Can't argue with that."

Bradbury finished his beer and plopped the glass down. "Well, it's been a pleasure talking to you, Mr. Prosper. I'll be in the office first thing. Come on by and collect your money."

"Obliged, Marshal."

"If you don't have a place to hang your hat while you're in town, the Clarendon House two blocks south and one east is a good one." He grinned. "They appreciate it when I send 'em business."

"Lousy pay even for the marshal, eh?" Prosper grinned too.

"Sad to say, yes. Better than many folks get, but I'm not getting rich. If you're of a mind for pleasures of the flesh, the Capitol is the place to go."

"They appreciate you too?" Prosper asked with a conspiratorial smile.

"Indeed they do. Fine women, good food, good whiskey. Ain't the fanciest in town but not far below it."

"Might have to wait 'til tomorrow on that one. Sounds like I'll need more cash than I can afford right now."

Bradbury fished in a vest pocket and came up with what Prosper thought was a coin. "I can't take money from you, Marshal. I can wait 'til tomorrow."

"It's not money. It's a token. He handed it to Prosper. "Clarissa, who runs the Capitol, will honor it. You can pay her when you've gotten your reward money."

Prosper grinned. "Now I'm really obliged, Marshal."

"You're mighty welcome. See you in the morning—if you've got the energy," Bradbury said with a laugh as he left.

Prosper departed soon after, checked into the Clarendon House, got his extra outfit from his saddlebags, and headed to the barbershop for a shave and a bath. Then he donned his clean clothes. The collarless striped cotton shirt and striped dark wool pants were no different than what he had been wearing except they were clean. He pulled on his worn but polished calf- high boots over his pants, dropped his dirty clothes at a laundry, and headed for the Capitol.

It was every bit as good as Bradbury had indicated and then some. The food was the best he'd had in a long, long time, the whiskey went down smoothly instead of burning a hole in his gut, and the auburn-haired doxy was skilled and attentive.

As he was getting dressed, Prosper heard a commotion downstairs. "Stay here," he said to his consort as he strapped on his pistol and left. At the bottom of the stairs, a husky man whose clothes were well-made and expensive but disheveled was shouting at Clarissa. The establishment's bouncer was unconscious on the floor. The man slapped Clarissa once, then again.

Prosper swiftly moved up behind the man and clouted him on the side of the face with both fists forming a club. The man sank to his knees.

Prosper reached down, grabbed the collar of the man's jacket, and helped him stand. "This man mean anything to you, Clarissa?" he asked.

"Only trouble."

"You want me to take him to the town marshal's office?"

Clarissa sighed. "Won't do no good, I suppose. The city fathers don't get too upset about someone whaling away on one of us painted ladies."

"Your bouncer there ain't a painted lady."

"No, but he works in a sporting house, which to the law is about the same thing. Guess you should just let him go. Bart'll be more alert if he comes back."

"I'll just take him outside. Maybe the air will cool him off, and then I can send him on his way."

"That'd be best. When he's gone, come on back. You missed your breakfast, and you'll get another night here free."

"I don't..."

"Hush. You deserve it. There aren't many men who'll stop another from beatin' on a whore—or a madam."

Prosper nodded. To the man, he said, "All right,

mister, let's go take a walk."

When they reached the street, the man snapped, his voice slightly mangled by a likely broken jaw, "Let me go, you damn saddle tramp." He tried to jerk free. Prosper spun halfway around and drove a fist into the man's stomach. The lout doubled over.

"I would suggest you refrain from any more such horseplay and insults, mister. I ain't above whackin' you a few more times to calm you down. You act like a man, not like some puddin'-headed oaf, and you'll walk away from this with just your jawbone cracked.

"I'll kill you for this."

"No, you won't."

"I'll have the marshal arrest you. A judge'll see you get time in the territorial prison for this."

"I doubt it, but I'll take my chances that any judge will see you for the walkin' manure pile you are and that I'm a decent fella."

"No judge'll do anything to me for beating a whore."

"That's probably true. On the other hand, not many judges will do anything to me for smackin' a jackass like you around whether I have reason to or not."

"You said you'd let me go. Where you taking me?"

"Down the street."

"Where down the street?"

"You'll see." Minutes later, Prosper shoved the man through the door of Marshal Bradbury's office. The lawman looked at him in surprise.

"You got a cell we can put this jackass in 'til he sobers up? We can get him a doc while he's 'resting.'"

"What's wrong with him?"

"Broken jaw, I suspect."

"What happened?"

"He ran into something that was stronger than his jawbone."

"You have anything to do with that?"

"Could be, but I ain't sayin'."

"He hit me," the man mumbled. Everyone ignored him.

"What was he doing when his jaw encountered this hard object?" Bradbury asked.

"Hittin' Clarissa."

Bradbury's own jaw tightened, but it was Armentrout who spoke.

"You brought this man here for beatin' on a whore?" he asked incredulously.

"She's a madam, not a whore."

"Same thing."

"And he knocked poor Bart unconscious."

"That don't make no..."

"Shut up, Ambrose. Why bring him here?"

"Figured the town law would just send him nicely on his way."

"I have no jurisdiction in this matter."

"Don't need you to arrest him. Just hold him for his own safety."

"From who?" Bradbury smiled, pretty sure he knew what was coming.

"Me."

"Reckon I can do that. Ambrose, go get the doc."

"But I don't..."

"Just do it, Deputy."

Angrily, Armentrout headed for the door. The man jerked free from Prosper's loose grip, shoved the deputy, and yanked the lawman's revolver out of its holster. He spun and fired once, tearing a small, bloody line across Prosper's ribs. As the man turned to fire at Bradbury, Prosper yanked out his own pistol and shot the man before he could get off a shot at Bradbury.

A pale Bradbury plopped into his chair. Armentrout stood, shocked, looking down at the man's body. It took only a few minutes for Bradbury to regain his composure. "Ambrose, go get Marshal Floyd and the undertaker instead of the doctor. Unless you need a sawbones, Elias?"

"I'm fine, but he ruined a good shirt."

Armentrout picked up his pistol and holstered it. He looked as if he were going to speak but said nothing and left.

"I'm in your debt, Elias," Bradbury said.

"Reckon not. If I hadn't brought this son of a bitch here, he wouldn't have tried to kill you."

"No matter, he did."

"I don't understand why he tried to kill you."

"Likely because he was drunk and I was going to put him behind bars for a while. He shot you first because you brought him here and had thumped him. I figure he thought you were out of the fight, maybe even dead, so he turned to me. It all happened so fast."

"Things like this always do."

"Reckon so. Anyway, I figured he planned on killing us all, so as I said, I'm in your debt."

"This gonna cause you any trouble?" Prosper asked.

"Doubt it. Town marshal's a friend and a reasonable man. Besides, he has no jurisdiction in my office. It won't matter so much why this fool was here, only that he tried to hit you, he shot you, and was planning to shoot me and maybe Ambrose."

CHAPTER 14

"You find out who that fool I shot last night was, Marshal?"

"Nope. He isn't from around here."

"Well then, I guess we won't know if there was any reward on him."

"More's the pity. You would've earned it. How was the Clarendon House?"

"Don't know, really. Seemed nice, I reckon."

Bradbury cocked an eyebrow at him.

Prosper grinned. "I spent the first night at Clarissa's, and to pay me for draggin' that bonehead out of there yesterday mornin', she gave me a free night there last night."

"Damn, how come I never get so lucky?"

"Your wife might have something to say about that."

"How'd you know I was married?"

"You look like a married man." Prosper laughed. "And you're wearin' a weddin' band."

"Sure you don't want to be a deputy? I could use

a man with a good eye like you have, and one who uses a gun like you do, too."

"Nope. Like I said, too much danger for too little pay."

Bradbury nodded. "So, what're you planning now?"

"I best go on my way and run down some other outlaws. That four hundred you just handed me won't last forever."

"Who're you chasing?"

"Clark Bascom, Gordon Munro, Mike Specter, and Mort Anglin."

"Nice group."

"Bad enough, I suppose. I've come across worse."

"I'd give up on looking for Munro for a spell. Got a wire the other day that he had robbed a stage near Julesburg a couple days ago."

"That'd give me a place to start."

"That's out there on the prairie a far piece. The redskins might still be on the warpath out there. Julesburg ain't far from Sioux territory. He's either brave or crazy. You'd be even crazier to follow him. Even if the Sioux, Cheyennes, and Arapahos aren't actually on the warpath, and there are reports that they are, it ain't unusual to find a few bucks out there raisin' hell on their own."

"Reckon you're right. I'm used to handlin' outlaws. Can't say the same about a war party. Know anything about any of these others?"

"Bascom hit a small bank in Georgetown, but with what he's worth, you're wasting your time. Anglin, though, killed a farmer and his wife up near St. Vrain, the Weld County seat. That's out there on the plains, too, but not as far into Indian territory. They were one of the few families left out there. Why they stayed around with all the troubles of late mystifies me."

"Sometimes a small patch of land is all a man has, and he'll fight to keep it."

"Didn't work this time."

"Often doesn't. But it doesn't stop men—and their women—from keeping at it. It's the way this country's been building since the beginning."

"I suppose you're right

"Where's this St. Vrain?"

"Northeast fifty, maybe sixty miles. Ain't much there."

"I've got no other place to start, I reckon. Which one of the mercantiles in town is the best?"

"All of 'em are good, but Slater's has the better prices."

"Obliged."

"Well, if you ever change your mind, you know where to find me. Good luck on your quest. Be careful. Some of these fellows are pretty hard cases."

"So am I, Marshal, so am I."

Within minutes, Prosper was in the general store picking up enough supplies to last him a week or ten days. While he had someone load the packhorse, he got his things from the Clarendon. Satisfied by the job done with the packing, he paid the man, saddled his gelding, and rode out of town with a wave to Bradbury, who was standing on the wooden sidewalk outside his office.

✳✳ ✳✳ ✳✳ ✳✳ ✳✳

St. Vrain was a small place, lonely and almost desolate. There were few houses and fewer stores, though there were three saloons. There was no marshal's office that Prosper could find. He dismounted in front of one of the saloons, tied his animals to the hitching rail, and went inside. It had a forlorn look about it as if it were a person grown old and weary. A dozen or so patrons sat at small tables, and a sleepy-looking bartender stood behind a bar that had seen far better days but now was dusty and sagging at one end.

"Whiskey," Prosper said. "Good stuff if you got it."

The bartender put back the bottle he was holding and picked up another. "Ain't too fine, but it's the best I got."

"It'll do." Prosper took a sip and didn't grimace much.

"What're you doing in our fine town, mister?"

"Tryin' to run down some miscreant who killed a family somewhere near here. Don't know if he's still around, but I figured this was the best place to start lookin'."

"You a lawman?"

"Unofficial."

The bartender grinned. "That's good. Means justice maybe doesn't have to be by the letter of law."

"Often works out that way. Sometimes doesn't."

The barman nodded. "Good enough to hear. Don't know his name, but he hit the McSween place a few days ago. Fellow farmer went by and found the bodies."

"Man and his wife?"

"That what you heard?" When Prosper nodded, the bartender continued. "Three kids too, boy and two girls. Oldest one was only nine."

"Damn."

"I'd use a stronger word, but I ain't that kind of fella. Anyway, Abe—he was the fella who come by—rode on to Hillsboro, five miles or so north. There's a tradin' post for farmers there. They have a wire. Must've sent notice down to Denver or Golden or both, I reckon, if you're here."

"I got word in Golden," Prosper said with a nod. He finished his drink and set the small glass down.

"Another?"

"Hell, why not."

"It's on me. A toast to the hope that you catch that son of a...that reprehensible scoundrel."

Prosper tipped his glass toward the bartender in a salute, jolted the shot down, nodded thanks, and left. There was still plenty of daylight left, so the bounty hunter rode on, following a barely discernible trail in the otherwise trackless stretch of prairie. He was beginning to wonder if he had gotten off the track somehow when he spotted his destination.

Hillsboro wasn't much bigger than St. Vrain, but it was in much better shape. There was plenty of activity even though it was almost dusk. It even had a respectable-looking hotel, along with four saloons, and, he assumed, at least one brothel. Along with the telegraph office, there was a bakery, a blacksmith shop, a fair-sized general store, a chophouse, and several other small shops. There was even a little adobe marshal's office, though it looked as if it had seen better days.

Prosper decided a night in a hotel would be a welcome relief from sleeping in a bedroll on the hard ground. And a real meal cooked by someone other than him would be a pleasant departure from his recent travels.

He checked into the Hillsboro Arms, then went to Bell's Chophouse.

He was eating his supper when a thin, post-middle-age man wearing a tin star walked up. "Mind if I sit?" he asked.

"As long as you don't expect me to pay for a meal."

"Marshal Tony Bowden." He held out his hand.

Prosper shook it. "Elias Prosper." When the marshal had taken a seat, Prosper asked, "So, what can I do for you, Marshal?"

"I'd like to know why you're in Hillsboro."

Prosper had never liked people prying into his business, least of all a scrawny tin star in a pissant town, but he saw no reason to be truculent. "Why do you want to know?"

"It's my business to know why a feller wearin' a fancy pistol rig comes moseyin' into my town."

"Just passing through."

"How long you plannin' on stayin'?"

"'Til I leave."

Bowden looked exasperated. "Got to make sure you ain't here to cause trouble."

"And if I was, you gonna stop me?" Prosper shoved another piece of beefsteak into his mouth and chewed slowly.

"I'd damn sure try."

Prosper looked at the lawman. He thought he could see nervousness in Bowden's eyes, but the man was fighting it. Prosper figured Bowden was just a small-town lawman trying to do his job, but he wasn't sure. "I bet you would, Marshal," he said evenly. "I'm chasin' a killer. I'd hoped to have run him down by now, but the son of a bitch ain't stayin' still."

"Who is it?"

"Nice feller named Mort Anglin."

"He the one killed the McSween family?"

"That'd be the one."

"Ain't seen him." He rose. "If I hear anything of him, I'll try to get word to you." He walked away.

Prosper watched the man leave. The exchange the two had just had seemed strange to him. Something was off about it. Bowden had been perfunctory at the end of the short conversation. Prosper shrugged and finished his supper. He spent an hour at one of the saloons, sipping a couple of beers before heading to his room at the Hillsboro Arms.

He was almost asleep when footsteps in the hallway stopped at his door. He rolled out of bed, grabbing his Starr from the holster hanging from the bedpost as he did. He knelt, arm across the bed near the foot of it, revolver cocked. He was glad he had locked the door as he always did in such a place.

Suddenly someone kicked the door open, and two men rushed in, stopping just inside the room. Both fired several times at the bed where Prosper's head and body would be if he were asleep.

From his position, the bounty hunter fired four times, putting two .44-caliber slugs into each man's chest. Both fell, half-in, half-out of the room.

Prosper rose and walked over to make sure the men were dead. One was Marshal Tony Bowden, the other was Mort Anglin. "I'll be damned," he muttered. "No wonder Bowden was interested in who I was chasin'." Even with the marshal dead, Prosper figured someone would be checking on the gunfight, and he wanted to be ready for whatever happened. He reloaded his pistol and tossed it on the bed while he buckled on his gun belt, then holstered it. He pulled on his boots, slipped into his black frock coat, and waited.

Soon, he heard footsteps on the stairs. Moments later, a Colt peeked out from behind the doorjamb. "Don't move," a disembodied voice said.

"I'm not going anywhere," Prosper said, standing in the center of the room, arms folded over his chest.

A couple of men nervously moved the bodies out of the way, and three men, guns drawn, entered the room. "I'm Deputy Les Myles. Gonna take you in 'til the judge decides what to do with you. Now, hand over your pistol."

Prosper opened his coat, hesitating for a moment while considering trying to take these three down. He was fairly certain he could do so even though they had the drop on him. Then he decided it would not be wise. There had been enough killing here, at least for now. Besides, if they'd wanted to kill him, they would have done so already or tried to. The bounty hunter gingerly eased out his pistol and squatted to place it on the floor at his feet, then rose and kicked it toward the three. One warily picked it up. The deputy waggled his six-gun and said, "Let's move."

As Prosper headed down the stairs, he had the sensation that this was not going to end well.

The marshal's office and jail were in a small ramshackle adobe. Myles escorted Prosper to a cell in the rear. There was no wall separating it from the desk and chair that comprised the office. The door hung haphazardly, and Prosper noticed that when Myles was locking it behind him, the door and lock were not very substantial. Such knowledge could come in handy, he thought.

CHAPTER 15

"When am I gonna get to see the judge?" Prosper asked the next morning when Deputy Myles brought him something that was supposed to serve as breakfast.

Myles grinned at him. It was not a reassuring sight. "Ain't really got a judge. We're just waitin' for Buck Anglin."

Prosper hid his shock. "He related to Mort Anglin?"

"Mort's brother."

"So that's why you didn't kill me," the bounty hunter said more than asked.

"Yep."

Prosper nodded. "How's Marshal Bowden fit into this?"

"Cousin of Mort and Buck."

"How about you?"

"Buck's brother-in-law."

"Regular family affair." Prosper paused. "When's Buck supposed to get here?"

"Likely tomorrow. Aimin' to escape?"

"Wouldn't you if you were in my position?"

"Reckon I would, but you ain't goin' anywhere, not with me and my two brothers keepin' an eye on you.

"I don't see 'em."

"They'll be here directly."

"Doesn't look good for me, does it?" he asked sardonically.

"Nope," Myles said with a malicious grin. He laughed as he went back to the rickety table that served as a desk.

Prosper quietly assessed the lock and began to formulate a plan.

Just before noon, one of Myles' brothers came in and took a chair across the table from Myles. They chatted of matters that were of no concern to Prosper, though he kept his ear open for any mention of Buck Anglin's pending arrival.

The brother left but returned around dusk, as far as Prosper could tell when the office door opened, with his other brother. The latter had a cloth-covered tray, which he carried toward the cell.

When he had heard the office door open, Prosper had eased his backup pistol—a .36-caliber Pocket Coltout of his coat pocket, grateful that those who'd arrested him had not thought to check for a backup. As the man neared the cell door, Prosper shot him in the throat. The man stumbled backward a couple of feet, then fell, dead. The tray and the dishes on it rattled on the floor.

Prosper slammed the heel of his boot against the lock of the cell door. It snapped, and the door opened a bit. Another kick fully opened the door. Prosper stepped through and shot Myles in the side of the head as he was turning toward the noise. It gave the other brother enough time to haul out his revolver and fire at Prosper before the bounty hunter put a slug in the man's stomach and another in his face. But the man's shot had hit Prosper in the meaty section of muscle just below the clavicle on his left side.

"Damn," Prosper snapped. He figured the bullet had gone through and had not hit anything vital. It hurt like hell, but he would not allow it to slow him. He quickly found his main revolver, checked to see that it was loaded, and holstered it. He shoved the cap-and-ball Pocket Colt back into his coat pocket.

Prosper cracked open the door and looked out. Dark was fast approaching, and the street was nearly deserted. He slipped out and, keeping to the deeper shadows, headed to his hotel. He edged up to the door and peeked through the window. No one was manning the desk, and Prosper figured the man was temporarily occupied elsewhere. He slipped inside and hurried to his room.

He slipped off his coat and hurriedly sliced a few strips from the sheet, pulled his shirt off his shoulder halfway down his arm, and with considerable effort, sweat, silent cursing, and will, managed to fashion a bandage to help stanch the flow of blood. He tugged the shirt back up and sat still for a few minutes, sweating, shaking, and breathing heavily. He reloaded the Pocket Colt from the powder, ball, and caps in a box he always carried in his saddlebags.

Finally he rose and slung his coat over his shoulder, then the saddlebags. The two helped cover the makeshift bandage. With the Henry rifle in hand, he headed out, hoping that if he strode across the small lobby, the man on duty would not recognize him. If he did, the bounty hunter would have to put him out of commission before he raised the alarm.

But he was lucky. The desk man was still away and Prosper briskly walked out, turning toward the livery stable. It was full dark now, and he was able to see only because of the half-moon and a blaze of stars. At the stables, he saddled and bridled his horse as quickly as he could, hampered by his wound. Then he rode out of Hillsboro, heading northwest. He figured that if anyone wanted to chase him, they would likely think he went toward Denver.

Through sheer grit, he rode through the night and much of the next day, stopping at last in midafternoon along a stream bounded by cottonwoods and willows. When he dismounted, he was shaky from pain, blood loss, hunger, and exhaustion. Still, he forced himself to care for his horse and managed to eat some jerky before falling asleep.

He didn't know how long he slept, but it was daylight when he awoke. Slowly, he gathered wood and built a fire. He cooked some bacon and made coffee and felt considerably better after he had eaten. He spent that night where he was, eating several times, then rode out the next day.

Just before dusk, he reached Laporte, a small place but bigger and more decent-looking than the forlorn Hillsboro. He stopped the first man he saw and asked, "There a sawbones in town?"

"Doc Carlson." He pointed after raising a cocked eyebrow at Prosper, which the bounty hunter ignored. "About halfway up the street here, left side, next to the hardware store."

"Obliged." Two minutes later, Prosper walked into Carlson's office.

A voice called from somewhere in the back, "Be with you right off."

Prosper plunked himself into a chair and leaned his head back, almost dozing. He jerked awake when someone asked, "Can I help you?"

The bounty hunter gingerly undid his makeshift bandage. "Need you to take a look at this bullet hole."

"Well, let me get your shirt off you so I can see what it looks like." When it was off, Carlson said, "Well, actually, you have two bullet holes, one in, one out." He seemed rather jovial.

"Is it bad?"

"Any gunshot is bad, Mr. ...?"

"Elias Prosper."

"Like I said, no gunshot wound is good, but you're lucky the bullet went clean through and didn't hit anything vital. Seems there's some cloth in it, carried there by the bullet."

"Is that bad?"

"It's not good. If you had gotten here right away, it wouldn't be a problem. After several days or more, I can still get the residue out. Have to knock you out, though."

"I'll stay awake."

"It'll hurt like hell since I'll have to dig through

the scabbing and such."

"I'll live."

"You mind if I ask how you got it?"

"I'd rather you didn't."

"Something like this'll be of interest to Marshal Digby."

"Figured it would, though I was hopin' to avoid it."

"On the run?"

"Maybe." When Carlson gave him a quizzical look, Prosper said, "I'm a bounty hunter. Got tangled up with some fellas, one who claimed to be a lawman. Reckon he was in that pissant town. Might be that folks there'll put out some paper on me."

"Best talk to the marshal right off. He's an honest man and a good lawman. If you've lived this long with this wound already, you'll live long enough to take care of business before I get to work on you." He grinned. "You might be less than sprightly after I'm done with you,"

"Thanks. I'll go see to my horse, get a place to stay, talk to Marshal Digby, then come on back here to have you work your magic on me."

"Some folks say I practice black magic," the physician said with a laugh.

Prosper was glad Carlson had slipped the shirt off his shoulder rather than cutting it off. That way, it didn't look too bad, and he could cover it with his coat if need be.

"Two stables in town, Barnes' and McPhee's. The former is just down the street here, the latter at the north end of town. McPhee's is a bit farther, but Art'll treat your horse right. Two hotels, both on Main Street. Can't miss 'em. Both are about the same as to quality. Also, there's Mrs. Alison's boarding house over on Prairie Street. She runs a nice respectable place. Young widow who could always use the cash. Marshal's office is right across the street from here. I'll send someone to find him to let him know you'll be by." The last was more of a question than a statement.

"Be obliged." Prosper rose. "Be back soon's I can, unless the marshal throws me in jail."

"I'll be waiting, sharpening my knives and such." The doctor let loose another laugh.

Prosper shook his head and left. He pulled himself onto his horse, rode slowly down to Prairie Street, and stopped at Mrs. Alison's boarding house.

A tall, slender, attractive woman answered his knock. She was taken aback at the sight of Prosper.

"Pardon me, ma'am. Doc Carlson says you run a good boarding house, and I need a place to stay."

The woman started to speak several times but was unable to say anything. The look of fright was deep in her gray eyes.

"I know I look awful, ma'am, but I'll not harm you. Still, if you'd rather I left, I'll do so." He turned to leave.

"Wait," she said, voice quavering, and Prosper turned back to face her. "If Dr. Carlson sent you, I think it'll be all right. Room is fifty cents a day, seventy-five with supper, a dollar for supper and breakfast."

"I figure you're afraid to ask, but I reckon you'd like some cash upfront?"

"Yes," the woman answered.

Prosper handed her a gold eagle. "Should take care of more than a week with the two meals. I might not be here for supper tonight or breakfast in the mornin' after I see the doc to get some work done."

"All right."

Prosper smiled through the stubble on his face and was glad to see that she relaxed a bit. "Mind if I put my gear in my room before I head to the stable?"

"No, please. Where are my manners?" She held the door open.

Prosper got his saddlebags and the Henry and followed Mrs. Alison to the room. It had a good-sized bed with a thick comforter and nightstand on each side of the bed, a small table with two comfortable chairs, and a bureau atop which sat a pitcher and bowl, along with a towel and some soap.

"I hope you like it." Mrs. Alison still sounded nervous.

"It's a fine, fine room, Mrs. Alison. Tell you the truth, if all the rooms are this nice, you should be chargin' folks more."

Once more, he wearily climbed into the saddle and rode to the livery stable, where he was greeted by Art McPhee.

"My horse's been ridden hard of late and not cared for as well as he should've been. I'm ailin' some, so I've been somewhat lax. I got an appointment with Doc Carlson to see about gettin' fixed up. Doc says you'll take mighty good care of the gelding here."

"I will. Any idea how long you'll need me to keep him?"

Prosper shook his head. "Can't say." He pulled out a double eagle and handed it to McPhee. "That cover me for a few days?"

"Yep."

"Obliged." Prosper trudged back down the street to the marshal's office.

The door was locked, but a lean middle-aged man wearing a badge came up a minute later. "Marshal Amos Digby," the lawman said. "Doc Carlson sent someone to tell me you'd show up. Said you had trouble somewhere."

"I did. Figured I'd talk to you about it. Doc says you're a good lawman, an honest one."

"Ain't all lawmen honest?"

"I'd venture to say there are some who would not pass an honesty test."

Digby nodded. "That's a fact. Makes us good ones look bad. Well, c'mon in." He unlocked the office door and went inside.

Unlike the place in Hillsboro, this one looked the way a real lawman's office should.

Digby took his seat behind his desk and indicated the chair across from him. After Prosper sat, Digby asked, "So, what's your story?"

CHAPTER 16

"No story, Marshal, just the facts. I'm a bounty hunter. I was chasin' a miscreant named Mort Anglin."

"He the one killed the McSweens?"

"Yup. I rode into Hillsboro, where I had heard he might be. I was eatin' supper when the town marshal, a fella named Bowden, came in and asked me my business. I told him I was chasin' Anglin. No more was said about it, but little more than an hour after my supper, two men burst into my room at the hotel, guns ablazin'. I shot both of 'em dead. Turns out one was Anglin, the other Bowden."

"You know why they came at you together?"

"Found out Bowden is... well, was... Anglin's cousin. Deputy Myles and two other fellas arrested me and put me in a cell. Found out they were keepin' me there for Buck Anglin, the outlaw's brother, rather than a judge or a county sheriff."

"Damn," Digby muttered.

"Yup. Found out, too, that the deputy was Buck Anglin's brother-in-law, and his two accomplices were his brothers."

"What a tangled web we weave."

"You're well-read, Marshal. Anyway, I made my departure from their jail."

"Which, I assume, was not without complications."

"You assume correctly. There are now three less Myles brothers poisoning the countryside, but one of 'em managed to shoot me in the shoulder. It's why I'm seeing Doc Carlson."

"Hell of a tale." Before Prosper could protest, Digby smiled. "And one I believe. Now, you best get yourself over to the sawbones."

"There a telegraph in town?"

"Yes. Three doors down to your left when you leave here."

"Obliged." Prosper went straight to the telegrapher's office. "Need to send a message to U.S. Marshal Chester Bradbury in Golden."

"Easy enough. What do you want to say?"

"Anglin killed. Don't have body. Still due reward. May be Hillsboro paper on me. Squash it. Explanation later. In Laporte for now. Prosper."

Prosper paid and headed to Dr. Carlson's office.

✳✳ ✳✳ ✳✳ ✳✳ ✳✳

"You were right, Doc," Prosper said with a gasp. "It hurt like hell. I think I left fingermarks on your table."

"You're a tough fellow, Mr. Prosper, but my table's tougher." He smiled as he used a safety pin to piece back together the bounty hunter's shirt where he had cut it open to make it easier to get at the wound. Then he put Prosper's arm in a sling. "Best take it easy for a few weeks 'til it heals up."

"I'll try. Sitting around doing nothing ain't my way."

"Do the best you can. I'll have my assistant take you back to where you're staying." His eyebrows raised in question.

"Mrs. Alison's. Can your assistant stop off at a mercantile while he's helpin'? I can use some new duds, as you can plainly see."

"It's unusual, but I'll tell him to do so."

The assistant, Micah Jones, was not happy about the stop but didn't complain too much when Prosper bought shirts, pants, socks, and a coat and arranged to have them delivered to his room.

The landlady was shocked anew when Prosper arrived, his clothing a mess, dotted with blood, but she directed Jones to help Prosper to his room, where the bounty hunter plopped into a chair. As Jones prepared to leave, Prosper said, "Hold on." He flipped him a silver dollar. "Obliged, Mr. Jones."

Mrs. Alison stood in the doorway, a mix of fear and sympathy in her eyes and posture.

"I ain't drunk, Mrs. Alison, if that's what you're thinkin'. I was shot several days ago. Doc Carlson just patched me up."

"I'm not sure that's any better," the landlady said, her voice quivering.

"Probably ain't. But I'm no danger to you or your other boarders."

"Well..."

"I have a package of new clothes comin' from Oxley's if you'd be so kind as to let him in here."

"I will."

"One other thing. Is it possible to bathe here, or will I have to go to the tonsorial shop?"

"It's unusual, but considering your condition, I can draw a tub for you. I'll get you when it's ready." She hurried off, seeming to Prosper to be even more frightened.

"Damn," he muttered. Such a beautiful, and from what he could tell, caring woman, and he terrified her.

His clothes arrived just before Mrs. Alison came to tell him the bath was ready. He nodded and, carrying his new clothes, headed to a room off the kitchen. Inside was a fair-sized copper rub, steam rising from it. He carefully stripped, stepped into the tub, and sat, careful not to dunk his shoulder. He let out a pleased sigh as he rested his head against the back of the tub and relaxed. Finally, he started scrubbing himself.

When he finished and had dried himself off, he dressed, finding it difficult to do with one almost useless arm. He managed, though it took a little time, then opened the door and called for his landlady.

"Yes?" Mrs. Alison said as she walked up nervously.

"Got somewhere I can get rid of these?" He pointed at his old garments.

"I'll take care of it."

"No, ma'am. There's no reason you should be handling bloody old clothes. Just tell me where to take 'em, and I'll do so."

"Old privy out back," she said, surprised. "Will you be attending supper with us?"

"I'm hurtin' some and wouldn't be a much-liked visitor to your other boarders, but I'd be obliged if you could bring a plate to my room."

"Well..."

"Just this once, and the door'll be open the whole time."

"All right."

** ** ** ** **

Prosper was feeling much better the next day and ambled to the tonsorial parlor for a shave and a haircut. He was on his way back to his room when a messenger stopped him and handed him a telegram. The bounty hunter tipped the young man and unfolded the piece of paper.

"Reward waiting. No paper found. Asked marshal in Nebraska Territory to investigate Hillsboro. Bradbury.

He spent the rest of the day relaxing in his room. Mrs. Alison came by at one point and asked if he would like some tea. He mostly hid the grimace that arose. "Coffee maybe?" he asked.

"Of course." She left and returned minutes later with a cup and a small but full coffee pot.

She headed out, closing the door behind her, and Prosper spent some minutes staring at it, thinking about the woman who had just left. There would be a world of joy in that woman, he thought. He turned back to his coffee. She ain't for the likes of you, Elias Prosper.

He sat down to dinner with the other ten residents, and despite his having left his gun belt in his room, they looked at him with suspicion and anxiety. There were only eight others at breakfast the next morning and seven that evening at supper. He lingered after the meal, watching Mrs. Alison clean up with a mixture of joy and sadness. He finally stopped her. "Sit," he suggested gently. "Please."

With a questioning look, she did so after a few moments' hesitation.

"It's time I was movin' on, Mrs. Alison."

"But why?" she asked, surprised. "You've only been here a couple of days. Don't you like your room?"

"It's a wonderful room. I told you that the day I took it."

"Then why?"

"I seem to be scaring off your other boarders, and that's not good for paying your bills."

"But..."

"It's best this way, Mrs. Alison. I'll leave in the mornin'."

Sadness crossed her face as she nodded. It surprised him.

Prosper was out of the boarding house before breakfast, and minutes later, he checked into the Laporte House hotel. He had breakfast in the hotel's dining room, then spent much of the day in his room, resting and thinking about the slender, auburn-haired Mrs. Alison. He smiled when he realized he had never learned her first name. He also came to a decision.

The next afternoon, making sure he was freshly shaven and otherwise presentable, he stopped by Mrs. Alison's. It was a time she would not have boarders around, though she still would have more than her share of work. He hoped he wouldn't disturb her. He knocked hesitantly on the door.

She looked up at him in surprise. "Well, hello, Mr. Prosper. What brings you to my door? Looking to move back in?" She appeared to be hopeful, but the look swiftly vanished.

"No, ma'am. It'd still be bad for your business."

"Then what...?" Her voice trailed off.

"I know I ain't very refined for a fine lady like you, but I was wonderin' if you'd allow me to come callin' on you?" Though the words had come out all right, he was angry at himself for what he thought was tentativeness in his voice.

"This comes as rather a surprise. I'm not sure I..."

"I understand, ma'am. I hope you'll forgive this old fella for his presumptuousness. Good day, Mrs. Alison." He started walking away.

"No, wait, Mr. Prosper," she called. When he turned back, she licked her lips in worry and wiped her hands repeatedly on her apron. "As I said, your announcement was rather a surprise. I didn't mean to sound like I was saying no. I'm still uncertain. It's been a few years since Mr. Alison passed on to his Maker, and I've not had much chance to spend any time with another man. Didn't want to for a long time, then got busy with this place and didn't give much thought to it. The few times I thought about it, I wondered if another man would find me wifely material, having been married and all."

"Hell, Mrs. Alison." He paused. "Excuse my language. "You're a beautiful and industrious woman and still young. Any man in his right mind would consider you quite the catch."

"Well, thank you, Mr. Prosper," she said, blushing at the compliment. She sighed. "I have had unwanted advances, I must say, but I've managed to fend them off. It's worrisome sometimes for a woman."

"I wouldn't know about that, Mrs. Alison, though I think any man who tries to force himself on a woman is a cad at best and a devil at worst. Is someone botherin' you these days?"

Mrs. Alison hesitated, then shook her head. "No."

"I'm not sure I believe you, but if someone does bother you...other than me," he said with a small grin, "let me know, and I'll see that he doesn't do so again."

A look of horror crossed Mrs. Alison's face. "I won't be responsible for a killing, Mr. Prosper."

"That what you think, that I'll just go and gun some fella down for tryin' to make unwanted advances to you?"

"I... We... You... I..."

"I don't kill men just for the sake of killing, especially if what they've done ain't a big offense. I'm sorry you think that way of me, and I'm sorry I've asked to court you. I was mistaken in thinkin' you might be open to the notion. I won't bother you again."

Before he could turn away, Mrs. Alison grabbed his shirt sleeve and tugged. "I didn't mean to insult you, Mr. Prosper. I just didn't know what to think. You originally came here with a bullet hole in you, and talk around town is that you killed several men. You carry a gun in a holster, and that makes it look like you're a man who lives by the gun. It's frightening to a woman."

"I am a man who lives by the gun, and if that frightens you, perhaps I shouldn't be courtin' you." He smiled ruefully. "I should've had enough sense to realize that before now."

"I am frightened, Mr. Prosper, but that doesn't mean I'm against spendin' a little time with you. In a proper manner, of course. It will, I think, be interesting. You're a strange man. From the way you carry yourself and the stories I've heard, you are one tough fellow, yet here you are, seeming a little embarrassed that you might have offended me by asking to come calling on me. It shows a different side of you, one that a woman...well, this woman, anyway, could prize. So, yes, Mr. Prosper, you may come calling on me."

"Thanks, Mrs. Alison."

"My name is Agatha, Mr. Prosper."

"And I'm Elias."

CHAPTER 17

Prosper thoroughly enjoyed his time courting Agatha Alison throughout the winter, which had come on soon after they began seeing each other. He found her intelligent, strong-minded, and independent, as well as compassionate and beautiful. Despite the pleasurable time spent with her, after a winter of not doing much other than that, Prosper was getting itchy to do something, to be on the move. When spring announced its arrival, he paid a visit to Marshal Amos Digby, doing so with a mixture of reluctance and anticipation.

"You have any paper on anyone causin' trouble in these parts lately, Amos?"

"Tired of squirin' Mrs. Alison around town?" the lawman joshed.

"No, not at all. But I'm itching to ride after some miscreants. Sittin' around doesn't suit me, especially for several months."

"Fella named Angus Finley robbed the bank down in Evans a week or so ago. Heard he has friends and family across the prairie all around there."

"How much?"

"Only two hundred. Far's we know, this is his first bank robbery."

"Reckon I can handle that."

"Just make sure you don't take on his whole family like you did in Hillsboro."

"I'll be mindful of that. Anything on Clark Bascom or Mike Specter hereabouts?"

"Not lately. I'll let you know if I hear anything. You going out after Finley?"

"Reckon so."

"There'll be hell to pay when you tell Mrs. Alison."

"I know," Prosper said with a sour look. "I'd rather face Finley's whole family all at once than face Aggie."

Digby laughed. "That'll teach you to get on with some young woman."

"And you never have?"

"Well, once." Digby laughed some more. "Still married to her, come ten years this spring."

"Regret it?"

"Nope. Except when I get angry at the young'uns raisin' a ruckus."

They both laughed. Prosper took the wanted poster and headed out, dreading his next task, though he could put it off for a little while.

That evening, as he and Agatha were sitting on the bench on the porch of her boarding house, Prosper said, "I need to be gone awhile, Aggie."

She looked at him in shock.

"I have business to tend to."

"Killing business, I suppose."

"Only if it's necessary." He sighed. "We've talked about this before, Aggie. It's how I make my living. It's what I do for my food and whatever else I need in life."

"You could give it up."

"No, I can't. At least not yet. If I was to do so, I'd need some money put up 'til I could find something else to do with my life."

"I don't know if I could love a man...live with a man who hunts other men for money, Elias."

Prosper was silent, so Agatha added, "Don't you have anything to say, Elias?"

"Nothing I can think of, I suppose. I am what I am, and I do what I do. I can't change that. Not now. Maybe someday. Maybe even someday soon."

"Then I think it best you not come around anymore." She was angry, but she was crying, too.

Prosper could take the anger, but the crying was difficult. He sat there for a few minutes after Agatha ran into the house. Then he rose. "Damn," he muttered.

As he was riding out the next morning, after a poor night's sleep, he ran into Digby. "How'd it go with tellin' Mrs. Alison?"

"About as well as could be expected, which ain't very well at all."

"Sorry to hear that, Elias."

"Me, too." He paused. "Even though she's thrown me over, I still have feelings for her," he said, embarrassed. "I'd be obliged if you'd make sure she was safe while I'm gone."

"I will do so, my friend. Good hunting."

** ** ** ** **

Late in the afternoon, Prosper waited behind some trees along the creek on the trail off the main road to a farmstead half a mile away. It had not taken him long to spot Angus Finlay. The only place he could go without traveling much other than to see family was a trading post/saloon on the plains, far from most everything except some farms and small ranches. He had followed the robber to where he had stashed the money. That night, not fearing using a torch because it was away from any abode, Prosper had counted the cash. It came to more than two thousand dollars, which meant Finlay had spent almost five hundred.

So now he waited for the outlaw on the trail to his brother's farmhouse, where Finlay was and which Prosper hoped he would soon leave. He did not have long to wait before Finlay came into sight. The bounty hunter held off until the outlaw was within ten feet of him before moving into the trail in front of the man, his revolver in hand. Finlay jerked his horse to a stop.

"Howdy," Prosper said. "I'd be obliged if you eased out that six-shooter of yours and tossed it into the trees, followed by that Henry in the saddle scabbard."

"And if I don't?"

"I think you can figure that out."

"Reckon I can." Finlay started reaching for his Colt.

"Left hand," Prosper said.

Finlay almost smiled. He carefully reached across his body, eased out the pistol, and tossed it away, then did the same with the rifle.

The bounty hunter rode up next to Finlay. "Hold out your arms, hands together. I'd advise you to not try anything. If I have to knock you off your horse, then dismount to put these shackles on, I'll be one angry fella."

With a dejected look, Finlay held out his hands, and Prosper clicked the irons around his wrists.

"Now, where's the money?"

The outlaw's eyes lit up. "I spent most of it and gave the rest away."

"That so?" Prosper slipped a loop with a slip-knot around the man's neck. "Well, let's ride on. You first."

They moved out. When they reached the road that ran between Hillsboro and Evans, Finlay started to turn toward the former.

"Keep going straight."

The outlaw's shoulders slumped. "Could've told me you already knew," he called over his shoulder.

"Wanted to see if you'd 'fess up."

Before long, they arrived at the hollowed-out log behind some boulders where Finlay had hidden his loot. Prosper pulled out the sack containing the bills and some coins and hung it from his saddle horn. "Now we can head toward Evans."

The following day, as they were getting ready to leave their camp, Finlay swung his manacled hands at Prosper. The bounty hunter shifted away from the blow and plowed a fist into the outlaw's midsection, leaving Finlay struggling to breathe. Prosper waited for a few minutes, then helped the still-gasping Finlay onto his horse and put the loop around his neck again.

Two mornings later, they rode into Evans. The sight of a man with a makeshift noose around his neck being followed by a well-armed man holding the rope caused a little excitement.

A slender though muscular young man hurried up as Prosper and Finlay stopped, the former pulling up beside the latter. He was wearing a badge. "Well, well, well, it's good to see you, Mr. Finlay." He looked up at the bounty hunter. "I'm Marshal Harlen."

"Elias Prosper."

"Thanks for bringing Finlay in." He paused. "You find the money?"

Prosper noted that there was no avarice in his voice. "Most of it." He pulled the sack off the saddle horn and tossed it to the lawman. "Best I can figure, he spent about five hundred, give or take a couple score."

"Not a bad recovery."

An older, well-dressed, pompous-looking fellow rushed up. "That the money?" he asked. "And the robber?"

"Yes, Mr. Dartmouth." He looked at Prosper again. "This is Mr. Dartmouth, president of our bank here."

The bounty hunter nodded at the bank official, but the man was paying no attention.

"I'll take that money now, Marshal," Dartmouth said.

"No, you won't," Prosper interjected. The two men looked at him in surprise. "Not 'til I get the reward. I could've taken it out myself, but I didn't think it was right."

Finlay started to say something but shut up at Prosper's glare.

"Reckon that'll be all right," Harlen said.

"No, it isn't!" Dartmouth snapped. "That is bank money, and back into the bank it will go."

"You're the one who offered the reward, Phil. It's only right he should get it from the money he recovered."

"No. He can come to the bank tomorrow and file paperwork to receive it."

"Like hell, I will," Prosper growled. "I don't get the money now, I'll ride on out with Finlay here and turn him over to the law elsewhere. I can get my money there without having to beg for it, and I'll add some in for carin' for Finlay as we traveled."

Dartmouth glared at him for a minute, then through clenched teeth snapped, "All right, dammit. Give it to him and then give me the rest."

The lawman opened the sack, counted out a number of greenbacks, and handed them to Prosper. He then closed the bag and handed it to Dartmouth, who rushed off even faster than he had arrived. Harlen grinned up at Prosper. "There's an extra forty in there for expenses.

Prosper grinned too. "Obliged, Marshal."

"Well, let me get this miscreant inside." The lawman hauled Finlay off his steed, undid the rope from around his neck, and tossed it to Prosper. "Unless you're headin' out right away, I'll spot you a meal over at Rosalee's," he said. "But you'll have to pay for your own room at the Rocky Inn."

"You're on. Let me just stable the horses. What're you plannin' to do with Finlay's mount?"

"Likely sell it. He won't need it where he's going."

"He'll get out eventually."

"By then, that chestnut will be flea bait. Why? You interested in buyin' it?"

"Trying to get that two hundred back already?" Prosper laughed.

"I wouldn't charge you more than fifty, but stable owner Barney'd likely charge you more than the two hundred."

"Don't need an extra horse anyway." He rode off slowly.

Before long, Prosper and Harlen were sitting down to a meal, a heaping plate of pork chops and potatoes for each of them, along with cornbread and sweet butter and plenty of coffee.

"So why'd you offer to feed me?" the bounty hunter asked around mouthfuls of edibles.

"Pretty much as thanks for bringing Finlay in. Dartmouth has been riding me hard about letting Finlay get away with the robbery. Seems to think I can ride all over the countryside looking for outlaws. Got up a posse when it happened and rode out after Finlay. Chased him for more than a day, even though it was well out of my jurisdiction long before that. Dartmouth threatened to have me ousted next election."

"My bringing in Finlay change that?"

"Don't know. Not all the money was returned, though most was. It might keep him happy. Or maybe not. I'll see come election time. I have half a mind to tell him and anybody else who's interested that they can have the job. Let some other fool take it and have to deal with all the nonsense he and the rest of the City Council throw at me."

"Sounds like you're ready to chuck it all right now."

"I would if I didn't have a wife and a couple of kids. Got to think of their well-being before my pride."

"That's what comes with being a good man. Always thinkin' of others ahead of himself."

"Well, I don't know if I'm a good man, just a fella with responsibility. And that makes it hard to do what I'd like to do."

"You could always just shoot Dartmouth," Prosper said with a laugh.

"Now that you mention it, that might be a good idea," Harlen said, joining in the laughter. When that faded, he said, "You seem to be a good man. Appears like you can handle responsibility, too. Ever think of marryin', raising a family?"

"Thought that might happen recently, but she sent me packin'. Didn't like that I hunted men for a living."

"Most women don't. How long you been bounty huntin'?"

"Since I mustered out in '64. Went from shooting at Rebs to shooting at outlaws."

"Hard way to make a living."

"Reckon so. Maybe one of these days, I'll find me another line of work."

CHAPTER 18

"Gordon Munro kidnapped a young woman after killing her family, except for an older brother, who made it to a town and had a wire sent out to here and elsewhere, I suppose," Marshal Amos Digby said. "The girl's only sixteen. Name's Sarah Powell. You were interested in huntin' him down before, Elias. Still interested?"

"Yup," Prosper responded. "More so now since he's committed more murders and run off with a young woman. When did it happen?"

"Wire said late yesterday afternoon."

"Where?"

"Over near Hillsboro, place about five miles southeast of the town across the South Platte. Old adobe house, like many out here."

"Which way did he go?"

"Damn fool headed east instead of west, best we can tell, at least to start."

"Indians still causin' trouble out there?"

"Not nearly as much as a year or so ago, maybe,

but some hotheaded ones are still causin' hell out there, we've been told."

Prosper shrugged. "I'll be riding out soon's I can get saddled and load a couple days' worth of supplies."

"Meet you at Oxley's store. I'll have a sack or two with vittles."

Prosper nodded and hurried to the livery stable. Ten minutes later, he tied his gelding to the hitching rail in front of Oxley's and went inside. Digby was just picking up two canvas bags. "Bacon, sugar, coffee, some salt beef and pork, beef jerky, and buffalo jerky. You have a fry pan, coffee pot, and such?"

"Yup. Need one more thing, though." He walked to the counter and purchased two boxes of.44/40 shells, paying dearly for them. Then he and Digby went outside. Prosper hung the bags over the back of the horse and mounted.

"Good hunting. Watch yourself out there. Those Sioux, Cheyennes and Arapahos might have eased up considerably on raidin', but they're still not friendly folk."

Prosper nodded and kicked his horse into motion. He pushed hard but not hard enough to tax his horse too much. He needed to make time, but he didn't need to end up afoot because of carelessness. He finally stopped just before dark fell. With no wood or water nearby, he made a cold camp and ate jerky and drank water from his canteen. He also poured water from the canteen into his hat so the horse could drink. He hobbled the gelding and let him out to graze.

The next afternoon he came on the farmhouse. There was blood all over the inside, though the bodies had been removed, Prosper guessed by the townsfolk who had been alerted by the one son who had gotten away. The bounty hunter took the time to look for tracks, finally finding two sets of hoofprints heading east. He loosened the cinch and let the gelding drink from the large trough near the house. He filled his canteens, too. Then he tightened the saddle and rode out. Judging from the hoofprints, he figured Munro and his captive were in no hurry, which suited the bounty hunter just fine.

That night and the next were cold camps, the first again with no wood or water, the next under a light but steady rainfall. There was no wood here either, but with the rain, there was at least water for him and the gelding.

The rain had washed away the tracks, so it took Prosper some time to pick them up again. That afternoon he came upon another bleak farmhouse with a flock of vultures he sent circling high when he closed in. At first, he figured Munro had killed the family, for they would be dead with the scavengers soaring above. The arrows in the first body he saw fifty yards from the house proved him wrong.

Other bodies outside and those inside had been pretty well gone over by vultures, wolves, coyotes, and other scavengers. During the war, he had seen far more than his share of bloody, devastating savagery, but this was still heartbreaking, especially the three small bodies, one of them just a tiny pile of bones with a few bits of flesh stubbornly clinging to them.

Prosper stood there for some minutes. He was torn. Part of him wanted to give these people a burial, no matter how sparse; another part wanted to be on the trail again. He finally decided on the latter. There was really little he could do for these people, and he figured it was more important to track down Munro and the captive woman before they faced the same fate as these people had. Or, the outlaw might kill the woman.

He let the horse drink and found a little hay in the barn for the animal. While he waited for the gelding to eat, he decided he could at least prevent the bodies from suffering any more indignities. He laid them, or their bones, side by side in the house, then covered them with raggedy blankets he found. Finally, he spread coal oil over the blanket-covered corpses and tossed a lighted match on them. Minutes later, he was back in the saddle and following the trail.

That night, he camped under a solitary cottonwood next to the barest trickle of a stream. He found enough wood to build a small fire, which allowed him to eat bacon and some stale bread, but more importantly, he could have coffee.

Three hours down the trail the next day, he came to a herd of buffalo. There were hundreds, maybe thousands. He had seen such groups before, but this one was maddening because he would have to make his way through the herd, and that gave him considerable pause. One wrong move, and he would be trampled to mush. Besides, it would have had obliterated Munro's trail, and he would have to search for it once more.

"Well, let's see what I can do about that," he muttered. He pulled the Henry and dismounted. Holding the reins in his left hand, he knelt and fired at an animal feeding with its side toward Prosper. It took five rounds before the animal dropped, angering Prosper at his inefficiency. It took two more shots pinging off a rock and kicking up some dirt before the brown wave flowed swiftly off toward the northeast.

The bounty hunter kept the Henry in hand as he remounted and warily approached the massive beast, but the animal was dead. With a sigh of relief, Prosper put the Henry back into the scabbard, dismounted, and picketed his gelding. He pulled out a knife and walked up to the bison. He had never butchered one before but figured cutting out some meat couldn't be much different than doing so on a steer. He knelt and began slicing through the tough hide. It was far harder than he had figured, but he finally had a few chunks of meat wrapped in a piece of hide. Then he moved on.

It took more than two hours before he got through the trampled ground where the buffalo had been feeding, and almost as long to pick up Munro's trail again. He wasn't sure, but he suspected he was closing in on the outlaw and his captive.

He camped that night in a spot where it was obvious the outlaw had stayed. There was water, some grass, and plenty of firewood. He ate some of the buffalo meat, which he found was better than beef. As he waited for the meat to cook, he reloaded the Henry and made sure his Starr was loaded, all six chambers this time. Later, he honed the hard-used knife. Finally, he hit his bedroll and drifted off to sleep, certain he would catch Munro very soon.

A few hours after he pulled out in the morning, he saw a couple of riders in the distance. He smiled grimly, figuring it was his quarry. Then he realized that instead of an outlaw and his captive, the horsemen were Indians. Despite wanting to race off, he dismounted, and keeping the gelding between him and the warriors, he forced himself to walk slowly. He hoped that if the Indians saw his horse, they might think it was a stray mustang and ignore it. He did worry, though, that if they thought that, they might want to catch it.

He breathed a sigh of relief when he stopped in a large buffalo wallow. As he was standing there, he heard far-off gunshots. He walked down the wallow 'til he could see over the top. There was a little dust hanging in the air where the two warriors had been.

"Damn," he hissed. He mounted his horse and rode out of the wallow. He was glad there were small dips and swells in the land. He rode on slowly despite his sense of urgency. There was no telling if there were other Indians about. Finally the gunfire was loud, and he knew the battle was just over the slight rise he was behind. He swiftly slipped hobbles on the gelding, grabbed his rifle, and climbed the hump of land, crawling the last couple of yards until he was at the top and peering over the crest.

Four warriors were lying about seventy yards away, Prosper figured. They were firing single-shot muskets at Munro, who was in another buffalo wallow, shooting back with a Spencer rifle. Neither side was having any success. A young woman sat hunched over, desperately holding the reins of two nervous horses. The bounty hunter thought she was terrified.

"Time to end this nonsense," Prosper mumbled.

He took aim on one of the Indians and fired. The bullet kicked up some dirt but did not seem to bother the warrior. "Damn," the bounty hunter snapped. Trying to hit prone figures seventy yards away was not going to be as easy as he had hoped.

Prosper sucked in a deep breath and let it out. Resting his rifle on the ground to steady it, he fired again. A warrior jerked as the slug tore into his head. "Now, that's better." He took aim again but missed as he flinched when a bullet kicked up a chunk of ground to his left. "Son of a bitch." He fired again, and the warrior who had shot at him from a kneeling position and was reloading his cap-and-ball fusil went down. Prosper wasn't sure the warrior was dead, but he was out of commission. "How d'ya like that, boys?" he said.

The two remaining Indians jumped up, grabbed their dead companions, and ran off. Seconds later, they raced away on horseback. Prosper fired again but could not hit the fleeing figures.

Down below, Munro stood and looked up the hill. Even at the twenty-five yards or so, Prosper could see the man's grin.

"Don't be too happy, boy," the bounty hunter said quietly as he put a bullet into the wallow's wall next to Munro. "Drop your weapon!" Prosper shouted.

"Go to hell, whoever you are."

Prosper fired, and the slug hit the ground between the outlaw's feet. "Next one takes you out."

Munro started to turn toward the woman, gun rising.

Prosper fired, sending the pistol flying as the outlaw's upper arm broke. It was, he knew, a lucky shot. "I got more if you want, Munro. Now lay on your belly and stay there."

Reluctantly the outlaw did so, and Prosper started walking down the hill. He grabbed a rope from one of the horses the woman held and tied Munro's hands and feet.

"Hey, take it easy, dammit," Munro said, voice filled with pain.

"Shut your mouth, or I'll gag you." He walked over to the woman and knelt beside her. "You all right, Miss Powell?"

She nodded, eyes filled with fright.

"That's good. Now, I want you to go over to the other side of this rise here and get my horse. He's hobbled. Can you get those off?"

Sarah nodded again.

"Good. Go on now. I'll take care of these horses." When she hesitated, he said, "There's no Indians over there, and no outlaws either. You'll be all right."

Silently, she rose and started climbing the rise.

"You got quite a bit to answer for, Munro. What in hell made you ride it this way when you knew—or should've known—this is Indian land?"

"I've traded with the Arapaho before. I thought I could get safe passage."

"Just like that?"

"Well, I was gonna trade that little trollop to 'em for it.

"You're even a bigger idiot than you are a walkin' sack of horse dung," Prosper said and kicked Munro in the side.

Sarah returned with Prosper's horse, and he changed the rope holding Munro's hands to shackles. He undid the knots tying the outlaw's feet and replaced them with a slip-knot loop on one ankle. The bounty hunter helped the outlaw onto his horse and tied his legs under the animal's belly. It was not necessary, but Prosper helped Sarah onto her horse.

They moved out, riding three across, Munro on the right, Prosper in the middle, and Sarah on the left. And they moved fast. Angry warriors bent on revenge might be heading for them. Prosper considered continuing through the night, but he needed to fix Munro's wound, at least enough to keep him going, and Sarah looked worn through. They stopped where Prosper had spent the previous night.

Though it was risky, he had Sarah build a fire, and he set the last of the buffalo meat cooking and the coffeepot heating. While waiting for the food, Prosper splinted and wrapped Munro's wounded arm. Since Munro had not seen fit to bring a bedroll for Sarah, after eating, Prosper gave the outlaw's to her, leaving Munro to sleep on the ground. The outlaw protested until Prosper gagged him.

The next night, as Sarah was crawling into the bedroll, she asked, "Why don't you kill him?"

"I want him to face justice before a court, so everyone can see what a manure-heap of a man he is." Quietly, he asked, "Did he abuse you?"

Her tears answered him.

CHAPTER 19

"Where're you taking me?" Sarah asked as they rode on the next day.

"Hillsboro. That's the closest town to where your folks were...where the wire came from. Reckon you have family there or nearby."

"I don't want to go there."

"Why not?"

"Because people will...won't..."

"She's been defiled," Munro said with something approaching glee.

Prosper glared at him, which shut the outlaw up. "Where do you want to go?"

"I don't know. With you. Where people don't know me."

"You won't have anyone to care for you."

"I don't care."

Prosper sighed. This was not a good development. He could only guess at what she was feeling, nor could he fully understand her desire not to face people she was familiar with, people who would know she had been despoiled. He had a vague idea of what had been taken from her and a much stronger knowledge that it could never be given back. "All right," he said after a bit. "We'll go to Laporte, where I rode out from. It's a long ride, but if you're willing, that's where we'll go. I expect we can find you some help there."

"You'll never find help for her," Munro said with a laugh.

"If I were you, I'd worry about me, not someone else."

"I got no worries, pal. I ain't ever gonna face a rope."

"You keep flappin' your gums, and I'll guarantee you don't see a rope."

"You ain't got the stones to shoot me."

"You sure about that?"

Prosper's tone gave the outlaw pause, but then he said, "Yep. if you were gonna shoot me, you would've done so already."

"Take a look at your arm."

Munro glanced at the bandaged splint. "Hell, that don't mean much. You should've just killed me. I get the chance, I'll kill you without givin' a thought to it."

"Of course, I don't have to shoot you dead. Wouldn't bother me any to stake you out here for the wolves or coyotes or Cheyennes to finish you off in a rather painful manner."

"I wish you would kill him, Mr. Prosper," Sarah said.

"He'll get his comeuppance. I want him to face

the law and have his guilt shown to everyone before the law stretches his neck."

"I hope you're right." Her voice was wispy and blew away quickly in the wind.

** ** ** ** **

Five days later, they rode into Laporte under the curious gaze of most of the townsfolk. Prosper's eyes searched for Marshal Digby, Sarah kept hers downcast, and Munro stayed where he was, slung belly-down on the saddle, shackles on his hands and feet and an old piece of buckskin stuffed in his mouth and tied there.

Digby hurried up. "Thought you were lost for all time, Elias."

"Not too many problems. Had to drive off a few warriors was the biggest doins. That and havin' to shut Munro up to stop his jabberin'."

"He didn't give you any real trouble?"

"Nope. Of course, he never got much of a chance."

Digby nodded and turned his gaze on Sarah. Before he could say anything, Prosper jumped in. "We best get Munro here in a cell."

The lawman looked at him in surprise. The bounty hunter gave a slight nod toward Sarah, then shook his head. "Can you have someone fetch your wife?"

"Sure enough." He called to one of the many bystanders who had gathered.

While the marshal did so, Prosper untied Munro, then pulled the outlaw off the horse. The bounty hunter and the lawman helped the shackled outlaw into the marshal's office, then into one of the two cells.

Head still hanging low, Sarah followed the men into the office, moved a chair into the corner, and sat.

"I can't keep this scum in here very long, Elias," Digby said. "Folks here learn what he did, and I'll have a lynch mob on my hands."

"You could just let the mob take him and handle it."

"Reckon I could, but it's not my way."

"I know."

"Any ideas? Since this took place out in the territory, I don't have jurisdiction. Neither does the marshal in Hillsboro or the Weld County sheriff, for that matter."

Before he could respond, a stout woman of medium height came rushing in. "What's wrong, Amos?" she asked Digby. "Bud said I was needed here right off." Under the shock of dark-brown hair, her face was flushed from running.

The lawman nodded at Sarah. "This young lady has been through a hard time of late. A serious hard time. She needs a little caring for, at least for a spell."

"Well, now that's something this ol' gal can sure handle." She turned to the young woman. "What's your name, dear?"

"Sarah Powell." Her voice was barely a whisper.

"Well, come along now, Sarah. We'll get you cleaned up nice and pretty and fill your belly with some of Mother Digby's home-cookin'."

"Wait a moment, Betsy," Digby said. He opened the door and went out. "Go on about your business, folks," he shouted to the small crowd who still lingered, hungry for news of what was happening. "Go on, like I said. There's nothing for you to see here, just an outlaw come to face justice. Go on, go on." Digby gave it a couple of minutes to make sure the crowd dispersed, then came back inside. "All right, Betsy. Straight home, don't dawdle."

"No need to tell me that, you old sourpuss." But she smiled sweetly at her husband before escorting Sarah out.

"As I was saying... Well, asking, of course, before Betsy arrived, what're we gonna do about Munro?"

"I don't know. Let me think on it a bit. I'm trail-weary and need some cleanin' up and some decent food."

"Just don't take too long."

"Next week be good enough?" Prosper said testily.

"Get out," Digby snapped, far more worried than angry.

** ** ** ** **

Bathed, shaved, and with a full belly, Prosper went to the telegraph office. "Need to send another message to Marshal Bradbury in the capital."

"Ready when you are."

"Munro caught. Laporte law can't hold long. Ideas?"

"I'll get that right off," the telegrapher said, seeming eager.

With a hand on the doorknob, Prosper looked at the man. "Breathe a word of this to anyone, and you'll be sittin' in one of Marshal Digby's cells right alongside that outlaw."

The man gulped. "Yes, sir."

The bounty hunter went to a saloon he knew Digby favored and found the lawman there. After ordering a beer, he said, "I wired the federal marshal in Golden to see if he has any ideas on what to do about Munro."

"Hope he comes up with something. And damn soon."

"So do I, Amos."

The next morning, with some trepidation, Prosper went to Agatha Alison's boarding house and knocked on the door. Agatha answered, and her eyes reflected anger.

The bounty hunter was taken aback but asked, "Is Sarah all right? I understand Mrs. Digby brought her here last night because they didn't have room at their house."

"How dare you send that little trollop here to my respectable boarding house?" Agatha hissed. "I insist you take that harlot out of here and keep her with you as you've been doing."

Prosper clenched his jaws so hard his whole face hurt. It was some moments before he could speak, and when he did, it was in a dark, menacing tone. "She is no harlot. She was taken captive by a murderous outlaw and debased after watching that scum murder her family in front of her eyes. And she was almost killed by Indians, then had to survive several days' trip to here, sometimes with little food or water, all in the presence of the man who had despoiled her." He paused to take a couple deep breaths to try to calm himself. "But I'll take her out of here and see if I can get her a room at the Laporte House. Go on and fetch her. I'll wait out here."

"She went through all that?" Agatha asked breathlessly, her expression having shifted from anger to horror.

"Indeed she did, unless she rode off willingly with that scoundrel and is now play actin'," Prosper said sarcastically, his anger not having ebbed much.

"Oh, dear," the woman said, tears silently sliding down her cheeks. "I didn't know. I couldn't know."

"Of course you couldn't, but you could've thought I'd have the politeness not to send a woman I was courtin' here to you. But no, you just thought I was a wretched son of a...man with no morals or decency." His anger was growing again.

"I'm sorry, Elias," Agatha said, placing a hand on his arm. "I... I just..."

"Just go bring Sarah out here, and we'll both be out of your life."

"No, no! I won't. I can't." She was sobbing now, her tears a flood.

Prosper pulled his arm away from her hand. "She can stay here?"

"Yes, of course. And you..."

"I won't be back," Prosper said harshly. "Betsy will keep her at the house as she can and bring her back here nights. She'll check on her. Goodbye, Agatha." This was not a time when he would call her Aggie. He stomped away, fury, hurt, and sadness fighting for dominance in his head, heart, and soul.

He was in a foul mood when he spotted Digby

wandering around Main Street, keeping an eye on things as he was paid to do. When the lawman saw Prosper, he hurried over and handed Prosper a piece of paper. "Response from Marshal Bradbury."

"Digby explained. Bigger reward due. Bring Munro here soonest. Office pays travel when arrive."

"There's no train nearby, is there?"

"No. Stage from here to Denver, train to Golden."

"Can you hold Munro 'til tomorrow?"

"Should. I don't think anyone in town knows what he did to get him jailed."

Prosper nodded and went to the stage line's office to make arrangements. In the morning, he showed up at Digby's office, which was crowded with Digby, one of his two deputies, and two large, muscled young men.

"I thought Ludwig and Vandenburg might be of some help if Munro gets recalcitrant about getting on the stage.

"Thanks." Prosper went to the cell and shackled Munro, who was none too happy but whose protestations fell on deaf ears and whose resistance was feeble, considering his wound.

Outside, the outlaw stopped. "I ain't goin' a step farther."

Without a word, Prosper got a rope from the nearest horse, made a quick loop, and slipped it over Munro's head, pulling it tight. Then he let out a length of the rope and wrapped it around the saddle horn. "Walk or get dragged," the bounty hunter said harshly. He took the horse's reins and started walking, allowing Munro to follow however he wished. Whoever's horse it was did not complain.

When they reached the stage station, the outlaw's eyes widened. "No passengers?"

"Just me and you. I can ask Ludwig and Vandenberg to join us if you think you'll get lonely."

"But..."

"Just get in."

Munro once again balked. "I can't climb up the stairs, manacled the way I am."

Prosper nodded, and Ludwig and Vandenberg hoisted Munro up the stairs and into the Concord stage, which had had some special alterations made overnight.

"Obliged, boys," the bounty hunter said, giving each man a five-dollar greenback.

Prosper shackled Munro's manacled legs to rings bolted to the floor and his arms to a pole that had been added near the seat the outlaw would be using. The bounty hunter stuck his head out the window. "Let's go, driver."

Moments later, the coach lurched to a start. They stopped twice to changes horses, then a third time to eat and switch animals and drivers. Both bounty hunter and outlaw napped along the way, and less than eighteen hours after leaving Laporte, they arrived in Denver. Munro was housed in the city's jail overnight, while Prosper had a room and good meal at a fine hotel.

In the morning, sheriff's deputies manhandled the outlaw onto the train for the very short trip to Golden. Prosper shackled Munro to the metal rail along the back of the seat. Other passengers boarded, looked in horror at the man chained to his seat, and gave him and the bounty hunter sitting across from Munro a wide berth. The whistle blew, large plumes billowed out of the smokestack, and the train jerked into movement, accompanied by a chorus of squealing and hissing.

CHAPTER 20

"Fourteen hundred?" Prosper asked in surprise as he took the fat sheaf of greenbacks.

"Yep," U.S. Marshal Chester Bradbury said with a grin. "Eight hundred on the original reward for Munro, four hundred more for his latest atrocities, and two hundred for expenses."

"Sounds high, but I'll gladly take it," Prosper said, returning the lawman's grin.

"Got plans for all that largess?"

"Not really, but I'll figure it out." A dash of sadness flickered through him. Not long ago, he might have used that money to get married, set up a household, and maybe start some kind of business, but that was out of the question now.

Bradbury saw the look and wondered about it but decided it was none of his business. "I could still use another deputy, Elias," he said. "You could cover the eastern part of the territory. Even work out of Laporte if you're of a mind to."

"Oh, yup, send the new fella chasin' criminals

through hostile Indian land," Prosper said with a wry grin.

"I'd say there's not many other outlaws who'd be dumb enough to ride into the path of a couple of angry tribes. I expect most'll be bank and stage robbers. The latter, especially, often carry federal papers of all kinds as well as bullion, though not so much east of Denver."

"Like I said, too much work for too little money."

"That fourteen hundred won't last forever, and while a deputy's pay ain't the best, it's regular and reliable."

"I'll think on it." He grinned again. "It's mighty early in the day yet, but I could spring for a snort or two if you're up to it."

"I never turn down a free drink," Bradbury said, smiling.

Prosper thought that might be a lie. He had not known Bradbury long, but he would guess the lawman was not one to drink to excess. "Let's go, then."

Prosper spent a few days in Golden having himself a little spree, then bid farewell to Bradbury. He once again turned down the job offer, though he offered help if the lawman needed it on occasion, and headed back to Laporte. He wasn't sure he would stay there. While he had made some friends, there was no other hold on him now that Agatha had spurned him—and insulted him, something he did not think he could ever forget.

Figuring Marshal Amos Digby was making his rounds at this time of day, Prosper headed for his hotel room. On the way, he stopped in Oxley's mercantile to pick up a new shirt and found Digby there.

"Welcome back, Elias," the lawman said. "How was your trip?"

"Uneventful. Munro tried to wallop me a few times but couldn't do much in manacles and with a broken arm. Hired a couple boys in Denver, like Ludwig and Vanderhaven here, to help unload and load that recalcitrant son of a bitch from the stage to the train. Had someone in Denver wire Marshal Bradbury in Golden that we were almost there, and he met us at the station with two town deputies. Munro was pretty subdued by then. Not sure if he was really giving up, or if he thought to lull us into thinkin' he was no longer a danger and hoped to make an escape. Doesn't matter much to me anymore. He's Bradbury's problem now."

"Paid well, I suppose?"

Prosper search Digby's face for resentment or greed and found none. He grinned. "Quite well." He grew serious. "How's Sarah?"

Digby chucked his head toward the door and the two men walked outside. "I didn't think talkin' about such a thing is a good idea in front of a gossip like Edgar's missus, who was listenin' in from the back I'm sure." He paused. "Sarah's doing as well as can be expected. Betsy checks on her every day, takes her around town some, makes sure she eats proper. And Agatha's taking good care of her. Sarah keeps asking for you." The lawman grinned. "I think she's sweet on you."

"Damn," Prosper said, a sour look crossing his

face. "You find any of kinfolk of hers who could take her off our hands?"

"Nope." It was the lawman's turn to look unhappy. "That girl's been through a lot, so we can't just give her a horse and send her on her way. Betsy's a kind woman and doesn't mind caring for her, but she's got our young'uns of her own. And Agatha can't afford to have a room taken up by a boarder who's not payin'."

"Maybe she's got kin somewhere outside the territory."

"We can hope the Good Lord sends some our way, but that prayer might not be answered. But I'll keep sendin' wires. I suspect there's still some folks—good friends of her family, if not kin—in Hillsboro or that area could take her in, but they're shunnin' her because of what happened."

"I ain't surprised."

"Me neither, but it's no help to that girl. She needs some loving folk to tend to her, and so far, she's got none, thanks to that son of a bitch sittin' in a jailhouse over in Golden." His anger was growing. "Maybe you can talk to her. Like I said, I think she's sweet on you, so maybe she'll open up about kin somewhere far off."

"Doubt it. She wouldn't talk to me of such things when we were headin' this way after I found her. Don't see why she'd do so now. And if things were bad with Agatha before, they got worse when Sarah showed up."

"Speaking of Agatha and things between you, she's been asking about you."

Prosper shrugged uncomfortably. "Probably wants to lock her door if she knows I'm back."

"Doubt it. Maybe I'm speakin' out of turn here, Elias, but I think you should talk to her, give her another chance. You won't find a better woman in Laporte or many other places, I'd wager."

Prosper shook his head. "I best be gettin' to the hotel, check on my things. I'll deliberate on whether to talk to Sarah."

Digby watched sadly as the bounty hunter walked away.

** ** ** ** **

Prosper knocked on the door of Marshal Digby's house. A boy of twelve or so answered the door. "Is your ma in, Mark?"

"Yes, sir. I'll fetch her." He ran off toward the back of the house.

Betsy Digby came out moments later. "Oh, that boy," she said in exasperation. "Leavin' you standin' here in the doorway. Come in, Elias."

"Don't be hard on him, Betsy. He's just a young fella."

"I suppose. So, what brings you here today?"

"I'd like to speak to Sarah."

The woman's eyes narrowed in suspicion. "I'm not sure I should allow that." Her protective maternal feelings rose.

"Nothing sinister, Betsy. I figure I know how she feels about me, and I've no intention of encouragin' her. I just need to talk with her. Amos has been trying to find kinfolk without success, so I thought she might tell me of some relatives elsewhere who could take her in. I'd be obliged if you stayed while I talk to her." He smiled sadly. "That way, she can't take advantage of me."

"That'd be something to see. Big, strong fellow like you trying to fend off a mere slip of a gal." She laughed. "Go into the parlor. I'll get Sarah."

The young woman's eyes lit up when she saw Prosper but dimmed when she realized Betsy was staying in the room.

Prosper wasn't sure how to start since this was new to him, so he just plunged into it. "We need to find you a permanent place to live, Sarah." He held up his hand to stop her from saying anything. "I think you might have feelings for me, and I'm flattered, but I don't return those feelings. You're a fine young woman, but I'm too old to be your beau, and I don't want to take advantage of you in your delicate state. Do you have..."

Sarah fled the room. Prosper looked at Betsy. "I reckon I ain't much of a sweet-talker," he said sourly.

"I don't think anyone would be for her. All she wants to hear is that you care for her and are willin' to overlook what's happened to her."

"So, what do we do?"

"I don't know. I can keep carin' for her for a spell yet, and I think Agatha doesn't mind lettin' her stay there nights, but it can't go on forever."

"I know," Prosper said dejectedly as he left.

** ** ** ** **

Prosper set the newspaper he was reading on the table and pulled his Starr.44 when the knock came on the door. He opened the door so it was in front of him, hiding him. "Come on in," he said.

Agatha Alison entered the room, her eyes darting nervously around, and stopped a few feet inside.

Prosper came around the door, startling the woman. He holstered his revolver but did not close the door. "What're you doing here?" he asked, the harshness in his voice tempered by a rare softness.

"Came to talk to you." Her voice was unsteady.

"I'm not interested in anything you have to say, Agatha, so just turn yourself around and go on back to your place." He had trouble keeping the roughness out of his voice, and he cursed himself inwardly for it.

"Please, Elias. Give me a few minutes. That's all I ask."

The bounty hunter hesitated, then nodded at a chair. "Sit. Leave the door open."

"No," she said, closing the door. "This is not for the public to hear."

"Ain't you afraid I'll ravage you?" Bitterness had crept into his voice.

"No, Elias. You may be a hard man, one who has killed people, but I don't think you'd hurt me or any other woman."

Prosper shrugged. "Take a seat, then."

"No. I'll stand. I think it'll help me say what I have to say."

Prosper sat. "Say it, then leave."

"I love you, Elias Prosper. I have for a long time.

You scared me when you first showed up at my door. You were filthy, your shirt and coat were bloody, you had a week or more's stubble on your face. You smelled of dirt and sweat and Lord knows what else. Despite my fear, I thought there was something likable, maybe even something to love, inside you. It's why I allowed you to have a room." Agatha fought back tears. "I felt something for you even then."

"Sure you felt something. Fear."

"That, too." She tried to smile. "But I liked you as well, and that turned to love when you decided to leave because you thought you were driving away my boarders."

"I was."

"I guess you were. I didn't care, though, even if it hurt me financially. I wanted you to stay around, be near me. I couldn't tell you that. A proper lady wouldn't do such a thing."

"You're doing it now. Have you become a not-so-proper lady?"

"Desperation calls for desperate measures. I need you to hear what my feelings are for you, Elias. If that means people will talk behind my back because I'm behind closed doors with a man who's not my husband, so be it."

"You had an odd way of showing what you claimed to be affection for me when you accused me of bringing a scarlet woman to your boarding house."

"It's because I loved you, darn it all! To love you and see you bring another woman to my place tore at me, Elias." She could not hold back the tears any longer. "I couldn't see that she was a lost, frightened young lady. All I saw was a rival for your affections."

"You didn't hesitate to make the accusation."

"I couldn't." She paused. "Like I said, I love you and want you to know and understand that. And to know that what happened when you brought Sarah to my door was because I love you."

"All right, I understand," Prosper said noncommittally.

With a seeming effort, Agatha stopped her tears, then breathed deeply a few times to calm herself. Then she began unfastening the buttons of her bodice.

"What in the hell are you doing, woman?" Prosper snapped.

"I aim to show you my love for you in the most intimate way a woman can." Her face was pink, but her eyes showed determination.

"Stop!" Prosper said, leaping up. "Get out!"

"What?" Surprise and confusion laced Agatha's voice.

"You think you can somehow earn my affection by disrobin' and makin' me swear I love you, or you yell that I'm takin' unwanted advantage of you?"

Tears in her eyes, her face flaming with embarrassment, Agatha took a few steps forward and slapped Prosper across the face as hard as she could.

The blow shocked the bounty hunter, not that it hurt that much. It was because she had done it, and he did not know what to do.

Agatha suddenly leaned against him, arms around his midsection. "I love you, Elias Prosper. I love you."

Prosper smiled, not in victory but in joy. He

wrapped her in his arms. "And I love you, Agatha Alison."

They stood that way for a little while, then Agatha pulled away and began unbuttoning her bodice again.

"Stop," Prosper said, grabbing her hands.

"Don't you want me?" Agatha asked, worry leaping into her eyes.

"Oh, I want you all right. Badly. But this ain't the time. Not like this. When we get married will be time."

Agatha's face glowed. "Married? You mean it?"

"Yes, I do."

"When?"

"Soon as we can. I can't wait long to have you in a husbandly way. Now button yourself up, wash your face, and go on home."

** ** ** ** **

The afternoon wedding two weeks later was small and intimate. Amos and Betsy Digby were the witnesses, and Parson Becker presided. The three Digby children were present, as were a few townspeople. Prosper was uncomfortable in his starched collar and tie. Agatha was glorious in a simple hastily though carefully made evening dress of cream-colored silk. The ceremony didn't take long, and the participants enjoyed a lovely dinner specially prepared by the staff of Bigelow's restaurant. Then the happy couple went to Denver for their weeklong honeymoon.

At their stopover on the way to Denver, Prosper

tore off his tie and collar and breathed a sigh of relief. He had wanted to do so as soon as they had boarded the stage in Laporte, but Agatha had convinced him to leave them on, telling him she was proud to be seen with such a handsome, well-dressed man. Now, though, he would wait no longer, but that was as far as he went in disrobing. In the crowded waystation there was little privacy, so they to put off truly becoming husband and wife.

The next evening, in their room at a fancy Denver hotel, Elias took Agatha in his arms. "You still as willin' as you were that other time?" he asked with a smile.

"I am indeed, sir." She smiled too but then flushed. "My husband," she started and hugged him tighter when she felt him stiffen at the mention, "was... maybe you could say a free-spirited man in the seclusion of our...room, and, well, he encouraged me to be so, too. I hope that you will not be offended if I exhibit the same freedom with you when we... become husband and wife."

"Well, I reckon there would be many a man who would take offense at such a thing. I ain't one of 'em."

"I'm so glad that's true," Agatha said as she pulled his head down to kiss him. Then she showed him how glad she was.

CHAPTER 21

Agatha Prosper was not happy, not one teeny-tiny little bit. "I do not want you to go, Elias! You shouldn't. You can't!"

"You knew when we got married that Marshal Bradbury might call on me from time to time."

"You're not one of his deputies. He's the federal territorial marshal. Tell him to get one of his deputies to chase after outlaws."

"He only has three for the whole Colorado Territory, and they're all caught up in other things."

"Then they can let the outlaw wait 'til they're not busy."

"Aggie, this man killed a six-year-old girl when he robbed that bank in Central City. He needs to be brought to justice now, as soon as I can run him down."

"Yes, he needs to be brought to justice, but it doesn't have to be by you."

"I'm best to handle such a thing since the deputies are all busy." He did not mention that

Bradbury did not think his deputies were capable of bringing in a man like Mike Specter, so he had called on Prosper.

"Elias," Agatha said, trying to calm herself, "we've only been married for five months. Your gunsmith shop is doing well. We're respected by most everyone here in town. You're risking all that to chase after some darn outlaw."

"It's justice," Prosper responded lamely. "Besides, the reward will go a long way toward fixing up that house you have your eye on."

"The money won't matter one whit if you get yourself killed. What then?"

A small smile appeared unbidden on Prosper's lips. "Well, then you'll be the owner of a gunsmith shop as well as a boarding house."

Face red with anger, Agatha snapped, "Why, you despicable, ungrateful, unfeeling devil. I hate you! I wish I had never married you!"

Prosper stepped across the room to her and pulled her into his embrace. She only fought a little. "That's not true, Aggie, and we both know it."

"You get killed and I will hate you, and even when I die, I'll not want to be with you in heaven."

"It doesn't seem likely I'd be waitin' in heaven. I expect to be down below, where you'll have no place."

"You are incorrigible." She pushed away from him, angrily swiping at the tears that had slithered down her cheeks. "Well, go on then. Go on and chase some outlaw and get yourself killed. See if I care!"

Prosper put on his hat and frock coat and headed

for the door, then turned, stepped up to her, and kissed her hard. "I'll come back. I promise," he whispered. Then he was gone.

** ** ** ** **

It was more than a month before he did come back, dirty, trail-worn, hungry, and tired. It had been, he told his wife, pretty bad. Winter came early up in the mountains where Specter had fled. It snowed more often than not, though he was thankful there never was too much accumulation. And the cold was numbing, even with the bearskin coat he had gotten from Oxley's. He often went hungry and frequently had trouble finding enough forage for the horses. He had gone from town to mining camp to ranch, chasing a man who sometimes seemed to be a well-named wraith.

Prosper finally ran Specter to ground at a small, poorly made cabin. He had had enough and no longer had any intention of trying to take this outlaw alive. Specter had killed too many people, caused too much trouble, and robbed too many banks. He would hang anyway if Prosper brought the outlaw back to Golden. Better to have it over and done with here and now.

He lay in wait in the cold and wind and snow for some hours. Finally, Specter came out of his cabin to relieve himself. Prosper let him finish, then put a slug from his Henry rifle into the man's chest as he was walking back to his cabin.

Prosper made sure Specter was dead before tending the gelding. He put the animal in the small rope corral with Specter's horse, which he saddled. Then he threw Specter over the saddle and tied him down. At last, he went into the cabin and wolfed down some deer meat that was hanging near the fire.

Prosper slept for several hours, ate again, saddled his horse, and then, towing Specter's animal carrying his body, pulled out. He rode all night and arrived in Golden a couple of hours after daybreak. He had traveled far in his search, only to find his quarry twelve hours away.

Marshal Chester Bradbury was happy to see Prosper—and the dead outlaw. He sent his deputy to take the body to the undertaker's. "You look like hell," he said jovially.

"Still look better than you. I think." His smile was feeble.

"Well, go get yourself cleaned up, have something to eat, and get some sleep. You'll feel all the better for it."

"Nope. Best I can recall, train for Denver leaves in twenty minutes or a bit more. I plan to be on it."

"Lookin' like you do?"

"Yup."

"Come on inside a minute." When they did, Bradbury handed him a badge.

"You must be loco, Chester, expecting' me to take that thing."

"I ain't gonna swear you in. Just wear the damn thing. Railroad folk will let you ride free. Probably your horse, too."

"I can pay my own way."

"You're being hardheaded, Elias,"

"No, just cautious. It ain't that I don't trust you, but every time I see you, you try to get me to wear that thing for real. I ain't fallin' for it."

"Well, I'll still maybe call on you from time to time."

"Do all the callin' you want, Chester. The only answer you'll get is no."

"You getting soft since you got married?"

"Ya know, Chester, if I wasn't so plumb wore out, you'd be spendin' the next few weeks at Doc Carlson's. Just because I'd rather spend my time with my wife instead of roamin' around the mountains huntin' outlaws doesn't mean I've gone soft." He grinned. "I like touchin' something soft. Like Aggie."

"Can't say as I blame you. I'll wire the money to the bank in Laporte. That all right?"

"Yup."

"Like with Munro, the reward's gone up since he killed that little girl. Seven hundred, and I'll throw in a few hundred more for expenses."

"Obliged, Chester."

"And I'll wire Amos to have him tell Aggie that you're on the way." He laughed. "And to not be frightened when she sees what you look like."

"Go to hell, Chester," Prosper said, but he smiled. "Adios."

Leaving Denver, Prosper rode to the stage station midway to Laporte. He spent the night there and left on the stage in the morning, making arrangements for the gelding to be cared for there for a couple days and then ridden to Laporte

** ** ** ** **

Agatha was waiting for Prosper when he stepped off the stage. She rushed up and threw her arms around him. "Lordy, I missed you, Elias," she said into the shirt over his chest.

"Do I know you, ma'am?" he responded with a smile that she could see only when he pulled back to arm's length.

"Well, maybe not, mister. I was waiting for my husband, but you're much handsomer than he is. I think I'll keep you around, and by this time tomorrow, you will certainly know me." Her eyes sparkled as he bent to kiss her, both heedless of the crowd of travelers around them.

"Are you all right, Elias?" Agatha asked as they walked with their arms around each other. Her voice was worried and shaky.

"I'm fine. Just very tired, worn down some, and hungry as all hell."

"Not lonely?"

"That too, but not so much anymore. Be even less so after I've bathed, shaved, eaten, and slept a spell."

"I'll make sure of that."

"You're not angry anymore?"

She stopped, so he had to, and faced him. "Yes, I am. But I've come to realize that a man like you has certain expectations for himself, and I have to accept it. I think I have, but I don't have to like it. And if you do this again, I'll be flaming angry at you again, but I'll still love you." She tugged him into motion. "Now, let's get home."

** ** ** ** **

Prosper was worried about Agatha. She often seemed more tired than her work at the boarding house, much of it now taken over by two employees, could account for, and she was sick quite frequently. He mentioned it to Amos Digby, who had become his best friend, one afternoon when the marshal stopped by Prosper's gunsmith shop.

Digby laughed.

"This ain't funny, Amos," he said indignantly.

"Sure it is, Elias. Good-funny. She's with child, Elias. You're going to become a papa."

Prosper still didn't see the humor in it. He wasn't sure about fatherhood, had never really thought about it. What bothered him most, however, was that Agatha had not said anything to him.

When Digby left, the gunsmith closed up shop and went home, the one they had purchased two months ago to mark their eighth month of marriage. He found Agatha sitting at the table, her face pale as if she had just been sick.

"You don't look well, Aggie," he said, his anger dissipating.

"I know."

"Why didn't you tell me?"

Agatha's head snapped up, and she looked at her husband with something approaching fear in her eyes. "Didn't tell you I was sick?" she asked weakly.

"No, Aggie, that you are with child."

"I was afraid."

"Of what?"

"Of you maybe not wanting to be a father. Of you maybe not liking it because you couldn't go on any more of your adventures. Because..." She started crying.

"And how long were you going to go before telling me? How long could you have gone before tellin' me?"

"I thought I could wait 'til I didn't feel so sick all the time."

"Well, now I know. I don't mind. In fact, I think I'll rather like being a father."

"Thank you." It was little more than a whisper.

Prosper shook his head. He had never seen Agatha so sheepish, and it didn't sit right with him. Not knowing what else to do here and now, he left and headed to the Digby house, where Betsy greeted him and Sarah avoided him. The Digbys had managed to fit the girl into their house and lives.

"Come in, Elias. It's good to see you come by. Question is, why?" She smiled.

"Aggie's been sick for a few weeks now. I just found out she is with child. I'd be thankful if you could visit her now and again to help her through this. I ain't of much use."

Betsy laughed. "Neither was Amos. I'll be glad to guide her through these times."

CHAPTER 22

"So, how does dealing with an infant sit with you, Elias?" Marshal Amos Digby asked.

Elias and Agatha Prosper were enjoying supper with Amos and Betsy at their home, a frequent occurrence these days.

"Well, it ain't exactly the first time I've had to deal with an infant," Prosper said with a grin that indicated he had secrets.

The other three looked at him in shock.

"What? When?" Agatha demanded.

"I was coming back from California with a stop in Salt Lake City after chasin' down some outlaws when I come across a Ute baby floating in a basket on a lake in the south-central part of the territory. I took him in and went to find the tribe he belonged to. When I found 'em, they wanted me to leave the child out in the open so the wolves or coyotes would kill him."

"Damned savages," Digby sputtered. The two women vigorously seconded that comment.

"They said the baby was cursed. The people had been in a battle with the Arapaho, and some were killed. Others tried to get away in the lake and drowned, includin' the baby's parents. Since the little fella survived, the Utes thought him cursed—bad medicine, they call it. So they blamed him and wanted nothing to do with him. I forced them to send out a woman to care for the little guy until I could get him to someplace where he could grow up."

"Did you?" Betsy asked, eager for an answer.

"Yup. I remembered an old friend-he was an old friend of my pa's from the fur trappin' days, which is how I met him—near the Huerfano River. He has a place that's like a small town with workshops, farming, ranching, and such. People come to him for all kinds of help."

"He sounds mighty rich," Digby commented.

"Not rich at all, but he does well enough to support a bunch of poor families. He started raisin' cattle and horses, did a little farmin'. He knew wheelwrightin' and found a carpenter, a blacksmith, a saddlemaker, and others to work with him. Soon people came to him for all sorts of things. Many of 'em are dirt-poor, so he takes whatever they can afford to pay. He gets a fair amount from selling cattle and horses. He's married to a Jicarilla Apache woman, and they have several kids."

"Did the girl stay, too?"

"Yup, as did...

"You didn't mind that she stayed there?" Agatha asked, tension in her voice.

"Well, no. She was..." Realization hit Prosper, and

he smiled. "No, Aggie, I didn't mind. I looked at her as a young sister, nothing more."

Agatha relaxed.

"As I was saying, she and the baby stayed, as did her would-be husband, who had joined us on the trail."

"'Would-be husband?'"

They wanted to be married, but she had a husband, and while she was able to separate from him, there was still trouble with Painted Bear marryin' Smoke Rising."

"You sound like you miss those people," Digby said.

"Reckon I do, some. At least Smoke and Lives Again, the baby. I wouldn't mind knowing how the child's doin'."

"Do you ever write them?"

"I ain't much on letter-writin'."

They were silent for a bit, sipping coffee while Agatha rocked the baby in a small cradle beside her chair. Suddenly, Betsy suggested, "Why don't you go down there and see them?"

Prosper thought that over, then shook his head. "I can't leave Aggie and Davy. The shop, either."

"Take Aggie and Davy with you," Betsy suggested.

Prosper looked at Agatha, who, after a moment's hesitation, said, "I think I'd like that."

"Well, maybe we'll just do that." He looked at Betsy. "How's about you and Amos come along?"

"I can't do that," Digby said. "As marshal, I need to be here."

"Your deputies can handle things for a month

or two while you're gone."

"What about the children? And Sarah?" Betsy asked.

"Bring 'em. If me and Aggie can bring Davy, you can certainly bring your young'uns, and Sarah too."

The Digbys looked at each other. The wife nodded eagerly. The husband did too, but more soberly.

"Reckon it's settled, then," Prosper said. "We'll leave in three days.

Over the next couple of days, Prosper closed up his shop and asked a sometimes assistant to watch the place. Agatha gave firm instructions to the two women who had taken over the running of her boarding house. Digby made arrangements with his deputies. The one-time bounty hunter bought two small farm wagons, one for the Prospers and most of the gear and supplies, the other for the Digby family. Stout mules were bought to pull the two wagons, and Prosper and Digby each tied a riding horse to the back of his wagon. Supplies were purchased.

** ** ** ** **

The group moved along the path that divided the livestock on the west from the farmland of corn, wheat, beans, pumpkins, and peppers on the east before turning to go through the wide gates of the Higgins compound. They swung the wagons parallel to the front of the house, facing west toward the huge barn.

Amos and Betsy Digby took in the scene: the activity in the shops, the chickens pecking at the seed on the ground, the riot of playing children, now frozen in watchful silence.

As Prosper hopped off the wagon and helped Agatha down, John Higgins came out from his wheelwright shop, wiping his hands on a rag. A smile split his face when he saw who it was. Matilda came out of the house, followed by Smoke Rising. The latter saw Prosper and rushed to him to give him a great hug. He wrapped his arms around her to return the hug, then pushed her to arm's length. "Livin' here suits you, Smoke," he said with a grin. "You're happy?"

"Yes. Very."

Prosper did not see the furious look Painted Bear gave him from where he stood in the shadow of the carpentry shop.

"Ah, another young woman who wants my handsome husband," Agatha said, but she was smiling.

"Not just young ones," Matilda said, and she also hugged the gunsmith.

"This is my wife, Aggie, and our son, Davy. And these are our friends Amos Digby, the marshal in Laporte, and his wife, Betsy. Their children there in the wagon are Mark, Belinda, and Helen. The young lady is their ward, Miss Sarah Powell."

The children climbed down and bowed and curtsied to the settlement's owners, then looked around eagerly, watching the other children, who had gone back to their noisy games.

"Well, go on and join 'em," Matilda said. Mark, Belinda, and Helen rushed off. "Come on inside out of the heat," she said to the newcomers.

Everyone went inside, and John and the visitors sat at the long table. Matilda and Smoke Rising fussed in the kitchen area and soon placed two pitchers of lemonade and two plates of polvorones de canela on the table. Matilda and the young Ute joined the others at the table.

"So, what brings you down here all the way from Laporte...which is where, exactly?" John asked with a chuckle.

"North and a little west of Denver. I wanted to see how Smoke and Lives Again were doing." He paused. "Say, where is that little rascal?"

"Outside with the other children. He's not a baby anymore," Smoke Rising said. "He's four now."

"He's gettin' old."

"Hell, Elias, we're all gettin' old," Higgins said.

"Your English is much better, Smoke. These folks, as rustic as they may be, seem to be teachin' you well."

The Ute blushed.

"Besides, Amos and Betsy here wanted to see a real live heathen Indian, one that wasn't about to raise hair on 'em, as Pa used to say."

"I can always change my mind about that," Matilda said with a faux scowl that turned into a laugh.

"You still bounty huntin', Elias?" Higgins asked.

"Once in a while. Aggie's mostly got me domesticated. I'm a gunsmith now. Own my own place in Laporte."

"You always were handy with guns. Even before the war, if I remember correctly." Higgins rose. "Well, folks, those broke wagon wheels ain't gettin' fixed while I sit here being insulted by the likes of Elias Prosper. And Matilda." Higgins rose and headed out to more laughter.

A few minutes later, leaving the women in the house, Prosper and Digby went outside and wandered through the compound. They stopped by the carpentry shop. "Howdy, Bear. You're lookin' well," Prosper said.

"Go away, Elias." Painted Bear grunted.

"Haven't gotten any friendlier, I see."

"Don't see why I should, dressed in these funny white man's clothes, doing damn-fool white man's work."

"You learn a trade like this, maybe get yourself some schoolin', and you could make something of yourself, boy. Have a decent life."

"Bah. Leave me alone." Painted Bear turned back to his work, snarling and slamming tools around.

Prosper grinned as he and Digby walked away.

** ** ** ** **

The visitors spent a week and a half at the Higgins compound, with three days out for a trip by the two men to Pueblo for some supplies. After supper the night before they were to leave, after Sarah and the children had gone off to the parlor, Matilda said without preamble, "Sarah would like to stay here."

"What?" Betsy asked, surprised.

"She feels safe here," Higgins said.

"Safe? She doesn't feel safe at our home?" Betsy sounded irate.

"That's not true, John," Matilda said. "It's more that she feels accepted here, Betsy. After what happened to her at Munro's hands, she thinks the people in Laporte see her as dirty, as used goods. She doesn't think she'll ever find a husband, and she's getting to the age where she thinks she's almost too old for getting married."

"That's foolish," Betsy said indignantly.

"Not to her."

"We treat her fine, better than fine. Like she's one of our children."

"She loves you and Amos and the children. It's not you she has problems with. She gets sad looks from many of the people. Some women and men look at her in disgust, or at least she thinks so. But here she's more comfortable. Around here are people who don't quite fit in society, or what's called civilized society. Look at me, a Jicarilla married to a half-breed man. We have two Jicarilla children and others who are half Jicarilla and part white and part Shoshone. Other children are the sons and daughters of married people of different races: one parent Mexican, one white, maybe, or white and someone from one of the tribes. We have some Indians, as you white folk like to call tribespeople."

"But we..."

"You've come here and treated us well. Others in most other places don't. Most whites don't like Indians or Mexicans or half-breeds. There's no changin' that. And too many white folks look down on women who've been disgraced. It ain't Sarah's fault she was defiled, but other folks see her as tainted."

Matilda held up a hand to forestall any protest or comment. "I ain't seen it directly, of course, since I've never been in Laporte, but I've seen it elsewhere. It ain't very comfortin' to a young woman. I never encountered it myself, either, but I know what it's like to be seen as a mongrel, less than a real human bein'.'"

"I never saw people in Laporte treat her poorly," Betsy said. She was upset, angry, and worried.

"Maybe you ain't. Maybe nobody's ever treated her poorly there. But she thinks people see her as corrupted, and that's what matters to her."

"What'll she do here?" Betsy's voice was soft and pained.

"We got room here, and she is welcome. I reckon she's had some schoolin', so she can maybe help teach the young'uns. There's shared work with some of the other women around. She'll be fine."

Near tears, Betsy said, "You're pretty wise for..."

"An old Indian?" Matilda said, mostly in jest.

"No, Matilda," Betsy said, covering one of the Jicarilla woman's hands with one of her own. "For a woman who's still young. You're about the same age as me, I reckon."

"Not wise, really. Just experienced from being one who's not looked upon with favor in many places."

** ** ** ** **

As the two families pulled out the next morning, Betsy looked back to see Sarah waving from the Higginses porch. Though he couldn't see it, Prosper knew that sadness was etched on Betsy's face.

CHAPTER 23

Prosper handed Agatha the letter the postman had given him at his gunsmith shop. "It's from John Higgins." She looked at him in worried curiosity.

"Read it," he growled.

His wife started to do so, and disbelief crossed her face. "Painted Bear's run off with Sarah?" she said rather than asked.

"And Lives Again."

"But why?" Agatha wondered aloud, shock thick in her voice.

"Because he's a damned son of...a damned scoundrel."

"What does it mean?"

"It means I'm going after him. I can't let that no good...dung heap get away with that child. Nor Sarah."

"You can't, Elias. You've got two children of your own now. You can't go traipsing all over the countryside, chasin' after a ghost, even as evil as Painted Bear is and what he's done."

"I owe that baby, and I owe Sarah."

"No, you don't. The baby is—was—Smoke's to care for. And he's no baby anymore. He's five, going on six by now. And Sarah was John and Matilda's concern once she started living with them. She's not your responsibility. Neither is the boy."

"I didn't save that boy when he was barely a few months old to have him taken off by a villain like Painted Bear. And I didn't save Sarah from more abuse by that damned Munro to see her taken off by that damned Ute."

"How do you know she was taken off by him? All John says in the letter is that she's gone, as are Painted Bear and Lives Again. Maybe she ran off with him."

"You don't believe that, do you?"

"I don't know whether I do or not, but it's possible. If they want to be together, let them be. It's none of your concern."

"Might be true for Sarah, but that boy didn't decide to just up and leave with Painted Bear."

"But... Well, darn it! What am I supposed to do while you're gone for however long that'll be?"

"You still have the boarding house, and we have money in the bank. If you need help with the kids, Betsy will help out, as will others if you ask 'em."

"I don't want you to go," Agatha insisted.

"I know."

"But you're going anyway."

"Yes."

"What if you don't come back?"

"We've discussed that before."

"And if I don't want you to come back?"

"Then I'll not come back."

"You don't really care, do you?"

"I care very much. I love you, Aggie. I intend to come back unless you tell me to stay away, but this is something I have to do. I don't want to be away from you or the children, but I need to do this."

"Men are so darned stubborn. Foolish. Every darn one of you. And you most of all." She sighed. "You just better come back to me, alive and in one piece."

"I fully intend to." He pulled her into his arms. "I'm torn, Aggie. I ain't afraid of any man or beast, but I'm afraid of losing you. But if I have to so I can run down that son of a bitch, I'll live with the hurt. I'll be mighty sad, though, I can tell you."

Agatha ignored the profanity. "Just go and do what you have to do and come back to me." She rested her head against his chest. "I'll miss you, darn it all."

"And I'll miss you."

"When will you leave?"

"Soon as I clear up a few business things and get some supplies."

** ** ** ** **

There was no joy this time when Prosper rode into Higginsville late one afternoon. John and Matilda greeted him solemnly, a reception he returned in kind. Before long, Prosper had cared for his horse, and the three were sitting at the table eating their supper. The bounty hunter wolfed down the food. "Sorry, Matilda, but I'm mighty hungry," he said between bites. "Ain't had hardly any vittles, let alone a decent meal, since I left Laporte."

"Understandable, Elias," Matilda replied. If she weren't so angry and worried, she would've felt his attacking the food was a compliment. "You look like you've been ridin' hard and long."

"That obvious, eh?" He expected no answer and got none. He finally finished the second plate of chili con carne and cornbread and sat back with a third cup of coffee. "So, what happened?"

"Not much to tell you," Higgins said. "Got up one mornin', and the bastard was gone," he added, drawing no recriminations from his wife over the profanity. "So were two of my best horses and a colt. And of course, Sarah and Juan."

"Well, Lives Again...sorry, Juan. I can't help but keep callin' him Lives Again. He didn't have any say in it, but did Sarah go willingly with Painted Bear?"

"We don't know," Matilda said. "At times she seemed close to him, even though he and Laura were still together. Maybe he wanted her and she wanted him, and they figured they couldn't be together with Laura still here."

"Might make sense."

"All's I can say is that if it's true that the two of them wanted to be together, we're mighty glad Honus didn't kill Laura and just take up with Sarah."

"I'd have to agree. When did they leave?"

"Been near two weeks ago now," Higgins said. "Soon's we realized what happened, I sent out a couple of my workers to see if they could track 'em down. They followed tracks for a while but lost 'em just south of Pueblo."

"Did you expect your boys to bring him back? Or maybe shoot him?"

"Neither. But I thought if they could find Honus, they'd report back to me, and I'd get the law after 'em for horse theft. Folks 'round here, includin' me, don't take kindly to horse thieves."

"Nobody does, except other horse thieves."

"When my vaqueros came back with no news of the son of a bitch, I wrote to you."

"And I got here as quick as I could." Prosper leaned back and scratched the stubble on his chin. "Since he was headed west, I reckon he's aimin' to go back to his people."

"Or at least to familiar territory. It might be foolish to take Sarah back to a Ute village. He's got to know that many of his people won't like a white woman in their presence. At least one who's not a prisoner they could use to bargain with the authorities."

"Well, I've not known that fella to be all that smart at times. He lets his heart, or maybe his ass, rule his head, and that doesn't work out well a lot of times."

Higgins and his wife nodded. "You're going after them, I reckon," Higgins said.

"I didn't ride all the way down here to sit and hold your hands."

"Figured. Just wanted to make sure."

"I'll leave at first light."

"The room at the back is ready for you," Matilda said.

"Obliged. Anything unusual about the horses? Something I can follow if I come across 'em?"

"Only thing that might be detectable is that the

colt wasn't shod yet, so if you see tracks of two shod horses with one smaller one with no shoes, it might be them."

"Ain't much, but it's better than nothing. Now, if you'll excuse me, folks, I best get some shuteye if I'm going to be on the trail early."

"I'll have breakfast ready," Matilda said.

** ** ** ** **

Instead of heading north and then following the Arkansas River west toward Pueblo, Prosper headed southwest on a hunch. A day and a half later, he stopped in Colorado City for the night. He had found no tracks that he could follow and was beginning to wonder if he had made a poor decision by going in this direction, but he had to stay with it, at least for a while longer. With the Utes having signed another treaty reducing their lands again, they would be found southwest of here, and that was where Prosper thought Painted Bear would be heading.

He skirted the southern end of the Wet Mountains, then made his way through North Veta Pass. Two weeks after he had left the Higgins place, he rode into Fort Garland. He stopped, dismounted, and tied his horse to a hitching rail in front of the commander's office. He approached the private stationed outside the door. "I'd be obliged if you'd ask the commander if he'd consent to see me."

"And who're you?"

"Name's Elias Prosper, not that that'll mean anything to him."

"What's your business with the major?"

"I'll discuss that with the major."

"I reckon the major'd not be pleased being disturbed by a saddle tramp." The soldier grinned insolently.

"Be difficult for you to eat Army food, even as bad as it is, with no teeth."

"You dumb bastard, thinkin' you can do that."

His chuckle stopped abruptly when Prosper swung his pistol up and stopped at the last moment, resting the barrel against the soldier's chin. "Yes," he said simply.

"I'll tell the major you're here," the man said. He turned, knocked, and went inside when he was given permission. He returned a few moments later. "Major Wentworth will see you, sir."

"Thanks. You're a good-size fella, Private. You control that insolence, and you'll be a formidable man."

"Yes, sir. I'll keep that in mind, sir."

Prosper didn't believe him but didn't care. The bounty hunter entered the room and removed his hat, slapping it against his leg a few times to try to shake the dust loose. He ignored the look of disdain the officer gave him.

"I'm a busy man, Mr. Prosper. What can I do for you?"

"You had any trouble in these parts from a renegade Ute?"

"Not that I can recall. Why?"

"He ran off with a woman and child a few weeks ago. I've been chasin' him for a couple weeks. I figured he was headin' to his people."

"Can't help you. Now, if you'll excuse me." Wentworth bent to his paperwork.

"It was a white woman. She was abused by an outlaw a few years back. She doesn't need to be abused again."

"She resisted?"

"Don't know. It doesn't matter."

"If she was defiled once, it won't matter if she is so again. I don't have enough men to go chasing after one Indian. You're looking for him. If you don't catch him, one of the chiefs in whatever village the buck finds will use the woman to bargain for some extra food or something. We'll get her back then."

"You are one disdainful son of a bitch. I never thought I'd see an American soldier refuse to try to rescue a white woman."

"Get out."

With an annoyed shake of his head, Prosper turned and left, a little surprised that the door was not fully closed. Outside, the private whispered, "I just happened to overhear what you asked the major. We did have a report of a young buck raidin' a couple small ranchos west of here. One family was wiped out but the other drove the son of a bitch off, and one of 'em came by here to report it."

"The major go after him?"

"Nope. Just like he told you, it wasn't worth going after one buck just for killin' some Mexicans. I think he's afraid the Utes'll attack us here if he riles 'em up."

"Nice fella, the major."

"None of us here care much about some Mexicans

getting killed, but havin' a renegade Ute-or any Indian-runnin' around doesn't sit well." He grinned. "Most of us wanted a chance to kill him just so we can say we killed us an Indian."

Prosper shook his head again. He didn't understand people like the private or the major. Then again, he didn't know any Indians or Mexicans other than those in and around the Higgins compound and Painted Bear, of course, and he would be happy to kill the renegade. "How far west of here?"

"Six, eight miles, then south a mile or so."

Prosper nodded. "What's your name, Private?"

"Paddy Corcoran, sir."

"Pleased to meet you," the bounty hunter said, not truthfully. "Mind if I water my horse over at the trough?"

"I don't mind," the private said. "The major might." He laughed.

"I'll chance it. I always did like livin' dangerously."

Another soldier came wandering by, and Corcoran called, "Hey, O'Malley, slip a sack of oats to this fella here."

"What the hell should I do that?"

"He's chasin' that renegade Ute. Since we can't catch the son of a bitch, maybe this fella can."

"Right-o. Comin' right up." He hurried off.

"Obliged, Private."

"Just get the bastard. It'll mean one less of those devils runnin' around."

"I'll do what I can." Prosper led his horse to the watering trough. As the animal was drinking, O'Malley hurried up with a small burlap sack of oats.

"Ain't much, Mister," he said. "But it's the best I can do."

"It's more than I had a couple minutes ago. The gelding'll appreciate it."

Ten minutes later, he was riding out of the small adobe fort.

CHAPTER 24

The Hernandez family had, like many others in this area, been related to the Martinezes and were still mourning their slain kin. Since he was the only one who spoke fair English other than a word here and there, Ruben Hernandez had been the one to go to Fort Garland looking for help. He was angry when Prosper stopped by.

"Why should I talk to you?" he demanded. "Gringos don't care for my people."

"Don't paint me with the same brush as those fellas over at Fort Garland. If I hated Mexicans, I wouldn't be chasin' the son of a bitch who killed your folks."

"You don't want to revenge us. You just want to kill an Indian."

"Not any Indian, just this one."

"Not because he killed nuestros familiares-mi abuela, mi hermano, una tia, una tio, varios niños, dos hombres, tres mujeres."

"Not because of that, no, but it adds to the

reasons I want to catch him. He stole a woman and a child when he run off from the Higgins place a few weeks ago."

"On the Huerfano?"

"Yup. You know him?"

"Sí. He's a good man."

"That he is."

"You seek this Ute because of Señor Higgins?"

"Yup."

"Bueno. I hope you catch him. After he attacked us and we drove him off, mi hermano Jorge went to check on our family a few miles away. He found them all muerto," Hernandez said with a hitch in his voice. "Another brother, Carlos, and I tracked him for a while, but we lost the tracks after ten, twelve miles. He go northwest toward the mountains. Maybe he follows the Rio Grande. I think maybe so." He shrugged apologetically. "Lo siento. I can be of no more help."

"Can't be helped. At least I got another place to start lookin'. Anything different about the tracks?"

"No, just several horses and an Indian pony."

"He steal horses from your family?"

"Sí."

"He hasn't switched then, just added some stolen animals. Well, thanks, Mr. Hernandez."

"Are you in a rush?"

"I'd like to get back on the trail after Painted Bear."

"¿Tienes tiempo para comer? Do you have time to eat? Your horse could use rest too, eh?"

Prosper thought it over, but only for a few

seconds. "Sounds good, Mr. Hernandez."

"Take that gelding to the barn. There's hay and some corn and agua."

The bounty hunter nodded and rode the two dozen yards or so to the barn, where he unbridled the horse in a stall. He decided to keep the oats for somewhere on the trail, so he poured a little corn into a feed bag and fastened it over the horse's head, then he filled the small trough with water. He unsaddled the mount and brushed him down. Finally he removed the empty feedbag so the gelding could eat the pile of hay in the corner.

A few minutes later, he was inside the house.

The adobe home was illuminated by the candles the women had lighted, but they could not dispel the gloominess of the mourning residents. Still, the women fed him well—chili con carne, tortillas, thick coffee, and afterward, sopapillas covered in honey. He finally sat back, sated, though the hotness of the spicy food lingered in his mouth. "Gracias. It was muy bien."

Even the grief-stricken women smiled a little at his butchering of the language.

He rose. "Gracias, Ruben, for everything. I aim to get Painted Bear, and when I do, I'll remember you and your family."

"Adios, Señor Prosper."

The bounty hunter wasted no time moving up the trail. He reached the Rio Grande just before dark and made a quick camp, then had a decent meal of the tamales the Hernandez women had given him and coffee.

He picked up the trail the next day after some searching. It did, as Hernandez had suspected, follow the river northwest, though usually a little distance from it. He hoped he was catching up to his quarry.

** ** ** ** **

Prosper got the feeling that he was being followed. He worried that Painted Bear had circled around and was coming up behind him. The itch grew throughout the day, and he passed an uncomfortable night. The Ute was the kind of man who would sneak up on someone in the dark and kill him in his sleep.

In the morning on the trail, he grew more concerned, until finally, he had to confront whoever was following him. He smiled, thinking he might challenge some innocent traveler. Of course, there didn't seem to be much reason, if any, for an innocent traveler to follow this trail.

He pulled into the trees, and tied his horse to a ponderosa pine, and walked back to stand behind the cover of the thick foliage. He waited, growing impatient as time passed. He began to wonder if his instinct had been wrong, but he was reluctant to give up without making sure no one was following him.

A long hour and a half later, he heard hoofbeats and the faint sound of voices, and he tensed. Within minutes, Privates Corcoran and O'Malley hove into view. Prosper shook his head in annoyance. He did not need the complications of having the Army following him, but after waiting a little longer and seeing no others, he decided the two soldiers were not part of a larger force. He got the gelding and rode on, closing the distance between him and the soldiers. "You boys lookin' for me?" he asked as he stopped five yards behind them.

Corcoran and O'Malley jerked their heads around, hands going for their pistols until they saw that Prosper was sitting there with his revolver held in hand.

"Why would we be lookin' for you?" Corcoran asked.

"Don't know. You tell me."

"No need for us to be lookin' for you."

"Except maybe hopin' I'd lead you to Painted Bear so you could have the 'glory' of back-shooting an Indian. After back-shooting me first." He could tell by the glance the two soldiers gave each other that he had hit the nail on the head. "I suggest you turn around, go back to the fort, give yourselves up, and beg Wentworth for forgiveness—not that he'd give it to you."

"What for?" O'Malley asked.

"Desertion."

"We didn't..."

"Bullshit. But now that I think on it, maybe you'd be better off turnin' around and headin' east or north before you get to the fort and just keep on going. The Army doesn't look favorably on deserters, and you boys'd be in a heap of trouble. Now, toss your six-shooters into the trees and dismount."

"If we don't?" Corcoran asked.

"I'll shoot you dead."

"You ain't gonna shoot a couple of soldiers. That'd get you a necktie party."

"You boys are even dumber than you look. First off, nobody will know that you're dead, nor that I was the one who killed you. And second, if they found out, I'd probably get a medal for shootin' a couple of deserters. Now do as I say, and you might come out of this alive."

The two privates looked at each other, and their hands moved toward their sidearms in the flap holsters.

"Slowly, boys. And know that I'm a heap better with my Starr than you are with those Colts."

After a moment's hesitation, the two did as they were told and stood there fuming.

Prosper gathered the reins of the two Army mounts and rode off without another word, ignoring the epithets thrown his way. A mile or so farther on, he stopped, took the soldier's Spencers out of the scabbards, and bashed them against tree trunks. He rode on and stopped every twenty minutes to toss something usable from their saddlebags into the woods. He stopped one more time when he spotted a cliff beyond the trees. He tied the horses to bushes, unsaddled the Army steeds, and carried the saddles and saddlebags, one at a time, to the edge of the cliff and tossed them down. Another couple of miles away, he set the Army horses free, slapping them on the rumps in a meadow, and they galloped off.

The bounty hunter searched the meadow until he found the tracks of his quarry, which wound randomly through the trees, making them difficult to follow. But he persevered, and the next day, he found the remains of a camp that he estimated his target had used only the night before.

Prosper pressed on, moving quickly but warily, also weaving between the trees. The trail was difficult to follow on the carpet of pine needles.

** ** ** ** **

Prosper felt the bullet tear into his side just below the bottom rib and rip out through his back before he heard the sound of the shot. He managed to stay on his horse, yanking the reins to turn the animal to the right and dart deeper into the forest even as another slug thudded into one of the trees. Grabbing his Henry, he slid off the gelding and darted behind a tall ponderosa pine. It was not that thick, but it was the best he could find and would offer some protection.

A bullet hit the trunk not far from his head. "Dammit," he muttered. He dropped to one knee and carefully peeked out around the tree. Gunsmoke lingered in the air in and over a hackberry bush. It gave him a target, and he fired several rounds. He heard nothing that would indicate he had hit someone, and he cursed again.

He looked down at his wound. It was bleeding but didn't seem too bad. He wished he had some way to bandage it, but there was nothing to be done about it now.

Three bullets came flying from behind another bush. They were well wide of the mark, but then Prosper realized Painted Bear was shooting at his horse, which scurried away. The bounty hunter swung around the tree and emptied the Henry into the chokecherry.

Prosper began to sweat. A box of shells for the Henry was in his saddlebags, and he wondered how far away the gelding had run. He loaded five of the shells from his gunbelt into the rifle and waited. He didn't know what kind of weapons Painted Bear had. With the rate of fire, it was evident that he had at least one multi-shot pistol, rifle, or both.

Suddenly he heard horses galloping away. "Son of a bitch," he snapped. Taking a risk since the Ute had extra horses stolen from the Ramirez family and had possibly sent them running, he spun and raced toward where his gelding had fled.

He found his horse nervously cropping grass in the underbrush and breathed a sigh of relief. He grabbed his extra shirt from the saddlebag, folded the bottom, and placed it on his side, managing to cover both entrance and exit wounds, then tied the sleeves on the other side of his midsection to hold the makeshift bandage in place. Then he reached into the other saddlebag for the box of shells used for both the Starr and the Henry.

A shot rang out, and the horse dashed off again. Prosper tried to pull out the box, but it fell back into the saddlebag as the animal bolted. "Damn fractious beast," he snapped as he dove for the cover of a small juniper. "I ever catch you again, I'll send you someplace that'll turn your ornery hide into glue."

Squatting, Prosper pondered his next move. Unless Painted Bear had decided to leave himself on foot, he had sent just the stolen horses to flush him out, the bounty hunter thought. He did not believe the Ute would be that foolish. It was possible that he'd sent Sarah and the boy off, planning to catch up to them later, but Prosper didn't think that likely either.

The Ute did not fire again, and neither did Prosper. The bounty hunter thought that if he kept quiet, Painted Bear might think he was dead or incapacitated, which would suit him just fine. He also wondered if the Ute had run out of ammunition, which would be even finer, but he would have to find out.

Prosper rose slowly, trying not to disturb the juniper's branches and give himself away. He tightened the improvised bandage, then started moving slowly and carefully backward, keeping the juniper and then other trees between him and where he had last seen gunsmoke. He worked his way southwest, figuring to come around behind Painted Bear. As he walked, he tried to ignore the wound in his side.

CHAPTER 25

A twig snapped, and a heartbeat later, a bullet whizzed by Prosper's head. "Shit," he barked quietly but vehemently as he darted behind a tree. He surveyed the area ahead of him. The camp was set not in a glade but a spot where the trees were a little less dense. He could see three horses tied to a rope picket line. A fire was burning low, smoke curling lazily into the sky. Small piles of tack and supplies leaned against trees. Then he spotted Sarah and Lives Again cowering behind a chokecherry. He could not see Painted Bear.

Another bullet tore through the branches of the tree above his head. He jerked the rifle up and quickly fired three rounds at the spot where gunsmoke lingered. The bounty hunter saw a shadowy figure, unarmed, darting from tree to tree. He figured the Ute had run out of ammunition, and he emptied the Henry at the fleeing figure but did not hit him.

Prosper set the rifle against a tree and waited. Minutes later, Painted Bear appeared in the open,

Lives Again held in his arms with a knife against his throat. The boy was too scared to struggle. The bounty hunter walked out into the open too, pulling his Starr as he did. He was surprised that the Ute was dressed much like he was, though he realized he shouldn't be.

"Put that gun down, white-eye," the Ute yelled. "Or I kill the boy."

"You don't want to do that, Bear. You'll be dead a moment later."

"At least I'll die like a warrior, and you'll be known as a child-killer."

"Hidin' behind a child ain't no warrior's death. Besides, if you kill Lives Again, not only will I kill you, I'll also take your scalp. From what I've heard, a warrior who loses his scalp can't get to the Happy Huntin' Ground. You'll forever be wanderin' someplace where you got no people. Even others like you won't be able to see you. They'll have their own hell, just like you." He walked a little closer. "Let the boy go, Bear."

The Ute remained as he was, apparently thinking.

"Tell you what, Bear. You let the boy go, and I'll face you man to man."

"I got no pistol."

"I'll leave my revolver on the ground and face you with a knife, or bare-handed if you'd rather."

"How do I know I can trust you?"

"I've never lied to you."

While the Ute considered that, Prosper looked over at Sarah. "You all right, girl?"

She nodded, her face pale under the dirt. Her

clothes were trail-worn and filthy, and she looked tired.

"You go with this son of a...this miscreant willingly?"

The young woman shrugged.

"Want to stay with him."

She vigorously shook her head, her hair whipping from side to side across her face.

"He abuse you any?"

Her face reddened.

"You want to go back to John and Matilda's?"

"They won't take me in again." Tears started.

"You been there, what, a year now, maybe a bit longer, and you think those folks'd turn you away? You know they ain't that kind of people."

"I know, but..."

Before Prosper could respond, Painted Bear said, "Put down the gun."

"Let the boy go."

"You first."

Prosper shrugged and set the six-gun on the ground. If the Ute killed the boy, Prosper would have plenty of time to grab the revolver and kill Painted Bear. He had to take the risk that the Ute would not kill the boy, that his pride would make him come after Prosper. The bounty hunter breathed a sigh of relief when Painted Bear released the boy, who ran to Sarah. The two cowered together.

As the bounty hunter moved forward, he realized he had lost a fair amount of blood and was not as strong as he usually was. But it was, given his sense of honor, too late to back down now.

Painted Bear suddenly charged.

Prosper was slow but managed to get out of the way of the charging Ute, whose blade nicked the bounty hunter's arm. Prosper spun and whacked the warrior on the side of the jaw with his left fist, then swung his own knife at Painted Bear's throat. But the punch had knocked the Indian back a couple of feet, and the blade cut nothing but air.

Painted Bear came after Prosper again, wildly slinging his knife, driving Prosper back until the latter saw a small opening, and his own blade sliced a shallow diagonal through the Ute's shirt from the clavicle to the lowest rib. Blood seeped out. The wound slowed the warrior for a moment, but his mind assessed the damage and realized it was not that bad.

But the bounty hunter did not delay. He charged in, his blade slashing, searching for flesh to carve. He was beginning to weaken.

Blades clacked and rang as they struck each other. The men grunted as one man's arm blocked the other man's. Each managed to inflict a few cuts, none deep, on the other. Both were tiring, but Prosper more with the blood loss. He knew he had to end this soon, and he regretted having placed his revolver down. This was no time for honor, especially with what Painted Bear had done to Sarah and Lives Again and the threat he had made to the boy. His eyes flickered to the six-gun, which was not far away, and he allowed himself to fall back little by little under the Ute's assault, using trees for protection when he could.

He could feel himself slowing down, and he faltered once, receiving a slice on his chest because of it. Then he was tantalizingly close to his pistol. Painted Bear apparently knew it too, and he took a wild swing at Prosper. The bounty hunter slid out of the way, brought his blade around, jammed it into Painted Bear's midsection, and ripped upward.

The Ute tried to stab the bounty hunter in the side, but his arm would not work, and he dropped his knife. Prosper pushed the dying warrior away. Painted Bear fell, his life fading within moments.

Wearily, Prosper walked over to where Sarah and Lives Again huddled together, fear in their eyes. He knelt next to them. "Everthing'll be all right now," he said quietly. "We'll go back to John and Matilda's, and you'll be safe there. Painted Bear won't harm you anymore." He started to rise and found he couldn't.

** ** ** ** **

Prosper awoke slowly, wondering for a moment where he was. Then he remembered, and he fought down a burst of panic. Where are Sarah and Lives Again?" he thought, trying to push himself up.

Then the woman's face appeared. "Stay still," she said firmly. "I poulticed the wound and bandaged you up. You need to be careful you don't start bleeding again."

"A poultice? Where'd you learn how to find what to use and then make it?"

"Miss Matilda taught me some herb medicine and such. She cares for the people who live there and had me help her once I started learning."

Prosper nodded. "How long was I out?"

"About a day."

"How's Lives Again? And where is he?"

"You mean Juan? He's all right, sleeping just over there." She pointed. "He's still scared and worried, but he's young enough, maybe he'll forget all this."

"Would be a good thing for him. What about Painted Bear?"

"Had a horse drag him out a half-mile or so. I didn't want scavengers feasting on him right here."

"Good thinkin'. You have food?"

Sarah nodded. "And coffee. Honus—Painted Bear—took what he could from that family where..." She stopped, shuddering.

"No need to say more. Besides, that's all in the past. Not that you can forget it, but it's done and gone."

The young woman nodded, still choking back tears.

"Why'd he bring Juan with him? He never cared much for the boy."

"Said he was going to bring him back to his people to be raised as a Ute."

"Damn fool."

"Maybe, maybe not. He hated John and Matilda and had lost affection for Laura. Hated being there and didn't want Juan raised by people he thought were bad."

Prosper shook his head in sadness at the folly.

"Want to eat?" Sarah asked.

"That'd be good. I'll need my strength. We'll need to get on the trail soon. John and Matilda and

I'm sure many of the others'll be worried about you and Lives...Juan."

Within minutes, Prosper was supping on tamales and a soup he thought was made of piñon nuts. As he ate, he asked Sarah, "Did you go with him willingly?"

"No. I didn't fight it much, though. At first." Sarah hung her head, her long hair covering her features.

"What's that mean?"

"I was friendly to him." Her voice was distant and lost. "We were both outcasts, you might say. He took it in his head that I was in love with him. Then he grabbed me, and we went off after he grabbed Juan. I thought at first that it'd be a lark."

"You thought wrong, eh?"

"Yes," she said in a whisper. "It wasn't long before he...he..."

"Hush now. Like I said, it's over and done. No need for anyone to know anything but that he took you off. Don't tell anyone you left with him, only that he took you."

"All right."

Prosper finished eating. "Well, we best get movin'."

"It's too late in the day. Another night here won't make any difference. Better you should rest some more, start healing."

"Reckon you're right. I ought to take care of my horse, though."

"Long since done." Sarah managed a small smile.

"Obliged." The bounty hunter finished off a mug of coffee and then lay back down. He was asleep in moments.

** ** ** ** **

They traveled as fast as they could, staying in the saddle for long days, but it was still tedious, and it seemed the miles did not fall behind them all that quickly. Sarah turned out to be a proficient cook and was adept at caring for Juan. The boy was rather standoffish at first, fear in his eyes whenever he was close to Prosper, but the bounty hunter was patient, and the boy began to warm up to him.

They stopped at the Hernandez place, and Prosper gave the family both haunches of a deer he had killed. That and the decency he had shown them the last time he had been there got him, Sarah, and Lives Again a night inside and a couple of good meals despite the family being wary of having Lives Again in their abode. He might only be a boy, but he was still a Ute.

The next day, they gave Fort Garland a wide berth. Prosper smiled, wondering what had happened to Corcoran and O'Malley. Before reaching the fort, they headed north and were soon traveling through a bizarre landscape of large sand dunes in the midst of the mountains. They hurried across a pass out of that sandy land. From there, it was a relatively easy two weeks before they pulled into the Higgins compound.

Smoke Rising rushed out of the house and grabbed Lives Again out of the saddle before the horse had stopped. Prosper grinned through his grimy beard. "Someone might think you missed the boy, Smoke," he said, realizing for the first time that Juan's Ute name, Lives Again, was even more apropos now.

Smoke Rising smiled through her tears of joy and did not answer.

Matilda had followed Smoke Rising out of the house, and she fiercely hugged Sarah as the young woman dismounted. "We've missed you, girl," the older woman said.

"Really, after all I..."

"Hush. Now let's get you into the house and cleaned up. And I bet you haven't had a decent meal in ages." Her words faded as the two women walked away.

Smoke Rising was already rushing the boy out of the compound to her house outside the walls.

"Would've been nice for someone to greet me," Prosper grumbled good-naturedly as Higgins shook his hand and clapped him on the shoulder.

"If you had shown up a month ago, maybe we would have." He and Prosper shared a laugh. Then Higgins asked seriously, "Was it bad?"

"I've had worse. Got wounded, but Sarah tended it well."

"And Honus?"

"He won't bother anyone anymore."

"Good."

Prosper sighed. "I figure you will, but go light on the girl. She was made a fool of and abused considerably."

"Give no thought to it. You know Matilda, the mother hen." He smiled. "You look like you could use some food and cleanin' up, too. A night or two here, and you'll be as good as new. I reckon Aggie'll be glad to see you."

"Hell, I doubt she'll even remember me, I've been gone so long," Prosper said with a rueful smile.

"Oh, I reckon she will. She might be just a wee bit angry, though." Higgins laughed.

She was both glad and angry.

** ** ** ** **

A year later, another letter arrived from Higgins. With some trepidation, Prosper carried it home and handed it to Agatha to open. He could read it but was reluctant to do so, considering what had been in the last letter he had received from Higgins.

Her face clouded as she took it, but a smile appeared when she read it.

"Well, what's it say?" Prosper asked expectantly.

"Sarah's gone and got herself married. An Anglo fellow who knew Felix from his days at school in Santa Fe. Seems the young man, Arthur Crosby, came to visit Felix, saw Sarah, and was smitten. He courted her for a while, and then he proposed. Apparently, he doesn't care what had happened to Sarah before they met. Matilda—John may have written it, but it's Matilda's doing, I bet—says Sarah told him about her past, so there'll be no surprises. The young man is taking Sarah to California to work on planning railroads."

"Well, I'll be. I hope she finds happiness."

"Me too, Elias."

EPILOGUE

Prosper walked back to his house alone, having waved off his children and grandchildren. He needed this time to be by himself, though he would forever be alone now that his dear Aggie had gone to her reward. still, he had their offspring and their progeny.

The family—sons, daughters, husbands, wives, and grandchildren—followed him to the house, as did friends and other well-wishers. He put up with it, though he did not like it, and finally, just the family was there.

"You okay, Papa?" his daughter Millie, the youngest of his two sons and two daughters, asked, worry creasing her face.

"I'll be fine."

"But you're all alone now."

"I'm well aware of that, Mill. I will miss your ma something awful, but we had a good long time together. And we had you and your sister and brothers. You were a gift to us, your ma always said. I agreed." He managed a wan smile. "Except when Davy and Ian caused trouble, which was more often than not."

"We weren't that bad," Prosper's oldest son, Davy, said.

"Not usually, but there were times. Now, go on home, children, and take the young'uns. I'll be fine. Not havin' your ma here will take some getting used to, but I'll be all right."

"You sure?" Mille asked.

"I am."

** ** ** ** **

"How old are you, Grampa?" twelve-year-old Marty asked.

"Marty!" his mother Elena exclaimed, shocked.

"It's all right, 'Lena. I'll be eighty real soon. Can you count to eighty?"

"Of course I can." The youth was indignant.

"When did you and Gramma meet?" fifteen-year-old Nell asked.

"Would've been in '66 or maybe '67. She was a widow who supported herself by owning a boarding house." When he saw the look his two daughters gave him, he grinned. "A real boarding house. I took a room there, though only for a short time."

"Why?" Marty asked.

"I was scarin' away her boarders."

"Why?" This time it was thirteen-year-old Max who spoke.

"I was what was called a bounty hunter in those days. I chased bad men and brought them to justice for the reward money placed on 'em. Carried a six-gun in plain sight. It scared many folks."

"You still have your gun?"

"I do. And I carry it sometimes, though under a coat. And I practice. I'm still good with it."

"Did you ever kill anyone?"

"Josh!" his mother Millie snapped. "What a bad thing to ask your grandfather. I've a good mind to take a switch to you."

"Leave him be, Mill. I would've asked the same thing when I was his age." He looked at Marty. "But it's none of your business if I did or didn't, so I won't be givin' you an answer."

"Were you ever wounded?" Max asked.

"A few times, yup. Once by a couple arrows."

"Arrows! You fought Indians?" Josh asked.

"Yup, though only a couple times."

"You and Ma never said anything," Prosper's oldest son, David, said.

"Didn't see the need to. By the time you were old enough to hear it, it was long in the past. Your ma didn't want me to tell you, and she didn't know all the particulars anyway."

"Well, you could tell us now," Millie said, interest sparkling in her eyes.

Prosper sighed. "Well, I came upon an abandoned Ute baby that his people didn't want."

"Why?" Elena asked, stunned that people would not want a deserted baby.

"Doesn't matter. I got a young Ute woman to feed the infant 'til I got a place to leave him. A young warrior who wanted to be her husband but couldn't—tribal law, I reckon you could say—joined us. He wasn't the friendliest of fellas. On the way to the place where I was gonna leave the boy, we were attacked by some Arapaho. I took a couple arrows in the fight with them. It wasn't too bad, though it hurt a little."

"Then what happened?" Marty asked.

"We drove the Indians off and went on our way."

"What happened to the baby?" Millie asked.

"I left him and the young woman who had cared for him at a friend's place down along the Huerfano. Fella and his wife, John and Matilda Higgins."

"And the one who wanted to be her husband?" Elena asked.

"Left him there too, until he went bad."

"What do you mean, Pa?" his younger son, Ian, asked.

"Ran off with the boy and a young woman I had rescued from one of the outlaws I had chased. She stayed with my friends, too."

"What happened to them?"

"I left your ma here and went after him. Ma wasn't happy, but I went anyway. It was something I had to do."

"And?" Elena asked, anxious for the answer.

"And I took the woman and child back to the Higgins place."

"I'm glad," Elena said. "But what about the Indian who..."

"He wouldn't bother them again," Prosper snapped.

"Have you ever been back to see this Mr. and Mrs.

Higgins?" Mille asked.

"Not since '71, when I chased that renegade. Thought about it from time to time. Even wrote to them on occasion early on but never went to see 'em. I had business to tend to, and you kids come along."

There was silence for a bit, then Elena said, "Why don't you go see them now?"

Prosper thought about that for few moments, then shook his head. "Nah. Reckon they're long gone. John was older than me, and Matilda was about the same age." He grinned. "She's a Jicarilla Apache, by the way. Besides, I doubt Smoke Rising and Lives Again'd recognize me after all these years."

"Smoke Rising and Lives Again?" David asked.

"Lives Again is the boy; Smoke is the Ute who became his ma. They're probably not even there any longer anyway."

"I think they'd know you if they're still there," Elena said. "If you change your mind, Davy'll even lend you the Model T so you can drive down there."

"I'll be damned if I'll get in that contraption," he said to a round of laughter.

Prosper did think about it more and more over the next several days, and then he decided. The next morning, he loaded some supplies in his saddlebags and bid farewell to his surprised and worried children.

"Wait 'til tomorrow, Pa," Davy said. "We'll take the car. It'll be easier and faster."

"You'll be lucky if we make it halfway. There ain't many fuel stations the way we need to be going. Not many roads either, at least ones that horseless carriage of yours can use."

"But, Pa!" Davy's wife, Elena, said.

"Besides, you got a family to care for and a business to tend to. You don't need to neglect either just to escort an old man on some crazy, foolish trip into the past.

And with that, he was off, taking a trail he had not traveled in many years. Two weeks later, he rode into the old Higgins compound. He was taking it all in when a middle-aged woman came out of the house.

"Can I help you, Mister?" she asked, voice pleasant with an unidentifiable accent.

"Hope so, ma'am."

** ** ** ** **

"What's all the commotion?" an older woman asked. Then she spotted Prosper.

"Elias?" she whispered. Tears started to flow slowly down her dark cheeks from coal-black eyes.

"This man scaring you?" one of the men asked.

Ignoring him, the woman rushed to Prosper, who wrapped his long arms around her and began to stroke her long, now-mostly-gray hair as she held him tight.

"You all right, Smoke?"

She nodded into his chest. "Missed you." She sniffled.

"I missed you, too."

An even older woman grinned and pointed at one of the men. "You won't recognize him, but that there fellow is Juan, 'Lives Again' as you were so fond of callin' him."

A LOOK AT:
SHERIFF'S BLOOD ROCKY
MOUNTAIN LAWMEN BOOK 1

Jonas Culpepper is the no-nonsense sheriff of San Juan County in Colorado, patrolling the vast empty lands with his 200-pound mastiff, Bear. His dedication has won him the respect of everyone on the right side of the law. But he is a fierce and relentless foe of those who cross him or those he has sworn to protect. So when the Durango-Silverton train is robbed by Mack Ellsworth and his gang of villains, it is Culpepper's duty to run them down and bring them to justice. But his job is made all the more dangerous when his enemies include men on both sides of the law. And when Culpepper's wife is kidnapped, hell comes to San Juan County in the form of one enraged lawman.

AVAILABLE NOW

ABOUT THE AUTHOR

John Legg has published more than 55 novels, all on Old West themes. Blood of the Scalphunter is his latest novel in the field of his main interest — the Rocky Mountain Fur Trade. He first wrote of the fur trade in Cheyenne Lance, his initial work.

Cheyenne Lance and Medicine Wagon were published while Legg was acquiring a B.A. in Communications and an M.S. in Journalism. Legg has continued his journalism career, and is a copy editor with The New York Times News Service.

Since his first two books, Legg has, under his own name, entertained the Western audience with many more tales of man's fight for independence on the Western frontier. In addition, he has had published several historical novels set in the Old West. Among those are War at Bent's Fort and Blood at Fort Bridger.

In addition, Legg has, under pseudonyms, contributed to the Ramseys, a series that was published by Berkley, and was the sole author of the eight books in the Saddle Tramp series for HarperPaperbacks. He also was the sole author of Wildgun, an eight-book adult Western series from Berkley/Jove. He also has published numerous articles and a nonfiction book — Shinin' Trails: A Possibles Bag of Fur Trade History — on the subject,

He is member of Western Fictioneers.

In addition, he operates JL TextWorks, an editing/ critiquing service.

Made in the USA
Monee, IL
03 June 2023